TRIPLE THREAT

TRIPLE THREAT

MIKE LUPICA

Philomel Books

PHILOMEL BOOKS

An imprint of Penguin Random House LLC, New York

First published in the United States of America by Philomel, an imprint of
Penguin Random House LLC, 2020.

Copyright © 2020 by Mike Lupica

Philomel Books is a registered trademark of Penguin Random House, LLC.

Visit us online at penguinrandomhouse.com

Library of Congress Cataloging-in-Publication Data is available.

Printed in the United States of America

ISBN 9780525514916

1 3 5 7 9 10 8 6 4 2

Text set in Life BT.

This book is for Hannah Grace Lupica.

TRIPLE THREAT

PROLOGUE

ALL I WANTED WAS TO PLAY FOOTBALL.

This is what happened because I tried.

1

ALEX'S FATHER DENIED IT EVERY SINGLE TIME SHE'D ASK.

"I know you wanted a boy, Dad. It's okay, I get it," she'd tease.

They were having the conversation again, on their way to the Orville town fair in western Pennsylvania. They'd spent the afternoon at the Pittsburgh Steelers training camp in Latrobe, a couple of towns over.

"How many times do I have to tell you?" Jack Carlisle said to his daughter. "You were exactly what I wanted. It was almost like I ordered you from Amazon Prime. Free shipping and everything."

"Then answer me this," she said. "Why'd you give me a boy's name?"

Jack Carlisle breathed a deep sigh. "Your mom and I *didn't* give you a boy's name," he said. "We named you Alexandra. You're the one who wanted us to call you Alex."

Alex smirked at her dad from the back seat. She never tired of messing with him like this. And despite the sighs and head-shakes, she knew he loved it, too. It happened a lot when they were together. And they were together all the time. Jack Carlisle and Alex's mom had divorced when Alex was only four. Her mom moved to the West Coast to become a surgeon and remarried, leaving Alex and her dad in Orville. Alex had regular phone calls with her mom, but she was closest to her dad. They were two peas in a pod. They both loved sports, but they loved each other more.

Alex's dad was a Steelers fan through and through. He followed other sports, too. Just not as closely as football, and not with the same enthusiasm as he rooted for the Steelers. When Alex was around eight years old, her dad began to notice how much she loved running and catching balls, and throwing them most of all. He used to joke that sports were one of the few things he'd passed on to his child. That, and his piercing blue eyes.

Nevertheless, Alex was still convinced he'd wanted a boy. And she told him so now in the car.

"I'm a lawyer, and I can't even argue with my own daughter," he said, shaking his head like he did when the Steelers were forced to punt.

They were stopped at a light now. He used the brief pause to turn to Alex in the back seat and said, "You know how much I love you, pumpkin pie."

He had a lot of nicknames for her, so many that Alex lost track of them all. But "pumpkin pie" was the first one she could remember.

"I do," she said, giving him a playful wink so he knew she was joking. "Admit it, though. You would have loved me a *little* more if I were a boy."

He sighed, resting his forehead against the steering wheel. "Alexandra Carlisle."

"Call me Alex," she said, and her dad chuckled. She loved making him laugh. It made her feel as if she'd scored a goal in soccer or struck out a batter in softball.

They'd had a great day at Saint Vincent College watching the Steelers practice. Now they were heading back to Orville, because Jack Carlisle had promised to take Alex to the fair. Her dad had told her about a famous Steelers wide receiver, way back in her grandpa's time, named Jimmy Orr. Jack Carlisle explained that their town wasn't named after Jimmy Orr, but probably should have been.

It was already the third week of August. The Steelers were playing preseason games, and Alex knew that the National Football League now had strict rules limiting the number of contact drills between games. But that was fine with her. She enjoyed watching all the passing drills, particularly the amazing accuracy of the three Steelers quarterbacks, from the shortest handoffs to the longest deep throw. She never got tired of watching the running backs and receivers run their patterns with such precision, making their cuts to the inside and outside from almost the exact same points on the field.

More than anything, Alex loved watching the flight of the ball, perfect spirals finding their way to their intended targets.

At one point her dad asked her if she was getting bored.

"Are you serious?" she said. "This is my team in front of me. It's *our* team."

"It'll be better when they start playing season games," Jack Carlisle said.

"Yeah." Alex nodded. "And we're back at Heinz Field."

Her dad had a pair of season tickets to Steelers games, on the thirty-yard line, visitors' side of the stadium. Jack Carlisle said he liked it better over there, because the Steelers coaches and players would be facing them, even from the other side of the field. One ticket for dad, one for Alex. They went to two preseason games and eight regular season games every year. Then, fingers crossed, to a home playoff game or two after that. The preseason games took place in August, and even though the quality of play wasn't much, the weather was usually pretty nice. Toward the end of the season, though, western Pennsylvania could feel colder than Alaska.

Even so, Alex and her dad never missed a game.

Loving the Steelers was one of the things that bonded Alex and her dad. They were as close as a father and daughter could be, and Alex could never imagine loving anybody or anything as much as her dad.

"My football girl," he called her, and not just during football season.

The Orville fair was set up on the grounds of the local church. They'd parked their car in the lot, bought tickets, and walked under the balloon archway at the entrance. Now they made their way across the fair, the sun still high, with plenty of daylight left before they'd have to head home for dinner. Seventh grade for Alex wasn't starting for a couple more weeks. She knew all her friends were trying to milk those last precious days of summer vacation and dreading the first day of school. But not Alex Carlisle. The start of the school year meant that the start of the NFL season was just around the corner. Pretty soon, she and her dad would have their Steelers back. Alex was always a little sad when they broke camp at Saint Vincent, just because the college was so close to where they lived. It made her feel as if the Steelers were practically *living* in her neighborhood. Heinz Field, on the other hand, was more than an hour away.

Alex still liked football better when the games counted, no matter how many times her dad took off work to take her to training camp. She liked her own sports better when the games counted, too. Softball in the spring, soccer in the fall.

Soccer was supposed to start up the week before she went back to school. Alex was a good enough player. She was a right backer, which meant she mostly played defense. Everybody talked about her passing and her vision and her decision-making.

She was a good, solid player.

But Alex wanted more than that from sports. From anything, really. She didn't talk about her dreams much. Didn't talk about them at all, in fact. Not even with her dad.

But her biggest dream was this:

Alex Carlisle wanted to be great at something.

Her favorite teacher at school, her English teacher, Ms. McQuade, always said the greatest adventure of all was the journey to finding your passion.

Alex hadn't found her passion yet.

Oh, she knew she had a passion for football, and for the Steelers. But that was different. No matter how much you loved your team, you were on the sidelines watching them. From the stands or the sofa.

You weren't in the game.

Yeah, she told herself. *You are good at soccer. Really good. But not great.*

The previous year, Alex and her teammates had watched together as the United States women's team won another World Cup. She had secretly rooted harder for the star player she considered her namesake, Alex Morgan. Her passion was clear. So was Megan Rapinoe's.

Alex Carlisle wished she could feel that way about soccer. And as good of a pitcher and hitter as she was, she didn't feel that way about softball, either. Neither sport was her dream. But she had a dream all right. It was just out of her reach. Like trying to grab a star out of the night sky and drag it down from the heavens.

"Hey," her dad said. "Where were you?"

"What?" Alex said, pulling herself out of her reverie.

"I felt like you left me there for a second," he said. "I asked what you want to do next."

"Oh," she said. "Sorry. It's like you always say: my head was full of sky."

"So what *do* you want to do?"

Alex put her hands on her hips and looked around, getting a panoramic view of the place.

Then she spotted the coolest and biggest stuffed animal she had ever seen in her life. But not just any stuffed animal . . .

"I want you to win me Simba!" she said.

The Lion King was Alex's favorite movie of all time. She loved the original animated version and watched it over and over to the point where she had the whole thing memorized. When the new live-action movie came out, she had dragged her dad to the Orville Cinema the day it opened for the midnight screening.

They went back three or four times after that. One day she hoped to see the Broadway musical in New York City.

Of all the characters, Simba was her favorite. She thought Simba was the bravest. But more than that, Simba's story resonated with her. It took him a while to realize his own dream, about being king. Just like Alex was taking time to figure out hers.

Alex's love for *The Lion King* rivaled even her love for the Steelers.

"Dad," she said, tugging on his arm, "come on. You've *got* to win me Simba."

They'd already been to a booth where you tried to win prizes by tossing softballs underhand into a milk crate. That didn't quite pan out for Alex and her dad. They'd stopped at the dunk tank, where Jack Carlisle hit the buzzer, plunging one of Orville's high school seniors into the water. The students were raising money for a local charity, so it was for a good cause.

But in the next booth over, where Alex spotted Simba, you had to toss a football through a hole that looked barely wide enough to fit, well, a football. The odds were unfavorable, to say the least. On the wall, an image of a football player was painted with his arms up, as if receiving a pass. The hole was where the hands came together.

Jack Carlisle had once been the starting quarterback at Orville High. He wasn't good enough to play college ball at Penn State or the University of Pittsburgh. But he'd had enough of an arm to lead the Orville Owls to the league championship in his senior year.

"I've got no arm anymore," he said to Alex. "Heck, when we're playing catch in the backyard, you throw better than I do."

Alex knew he was right about that but didn't want to discourage him from trying to win her the enormous stuffed animal. It would take up the whole back seat of her dad's car. It was amazing. She couldn't leave the fair without it.

Jack Carlisle made a beeline for another carnival game, but Alex grabbed his shirt sleeve and pulled him back toward the booth.

"Come on, Dad," she said. "Aren't you always telling me the most important thing for a quarterback is hitting what they're aiming for?"

"Yeah, when you've still got the arm," he said. "I left mine back in high school."

"You've still got it!" she said. "Who'd know better than your favorite wide receiver?"

"I've still got it *in the backyard*," he said.

"Please, Daddy," she said, looking up at him with big, pleading eyes. She knew she was being dramatic, but it was fun to tease him.

"Oh, here we go with the *please, Daddy*," he said. "I'm assuming that'll be the same tone of voice you use when you want your own car someday."

"Today I just want a lion," she said.

It cost five dollars for three throws. The young man running the booth said that nobody had put a football through the hole since they'd opened that morning.

Now that they were standing at the counter, Alex understood

why. She was pretty good at judging distances. This was at least a fifteen-yard throw from where they stood. Maybe even a little more. She looked at the hole, then over at Simba, and thought:

Really big prize.

Really small target.

"You got this," she said to her dad.

"In your dreams," he replied.

Alex smiled.

If he only knew.

Her dad made a big circle motion with his right arm, giving himself a quick warm-up. He groaned as he did.

"Nobody likes a whiner," Alex said to him.

Her dad huffed at that. "You better hope I don't pull a muscle," he said, "or you'll be driving us home."

"Really?"

"No," he said, laughing.

The young man handed Jack Carlisle a beat-up-looking ball from a basket of them on the counter and grinned.

"I don't want you to think I'm betting against you," he said. "But my shift ends in half an hour, and I bet one of my buddies twenty bucks that nobody would make this throw today. Nobody made it yesterday, either."

"You can start counting your money right now," Jack said.

"Hey!" Alex said. "A little positivity couldn't hurt."

"More like wishful thinking," he replied.

Then he took his first shot.

The throw missed the player completely. He groaned even

more loudly than he had while warming up. "That was pathetic," he said.

"You said it, not me," Alex said, throwing her hands up in defense.

"Hey," he said, grinning. "Who's got the bad attitude now?"

His second throw hit the player.

In the knee.

"Getting closer," Alex said.

"That's your pep talk?"

Alex just shrugged, but flashed her dad a quick smile.

His last errant throw, to Alex's great amusement, hit the player right below the belt.

"Now *that*," the guy behind the counter said, "has *got* to hurt."

Alex couldn't help it. She laughed. Even though that last miss meant her dad had lost his chance at winning the prize.

"Oh, you think it's funny, hotshot?" her dad said, giving her a playful nudge. "Why don't you try?"

"You're willing to lose another five dollars?" Alex said.

"I've seen that arm of yours," he said. "Maybe I'm looking to *win* a bet. Even if it costs our friend here his."

"It's on," Alex said.

Her light brown ponytail was sticking out of the opening in the back of her black-and-gold Steelers cap. She removed it so she'd have a clear view of the target. Then she secured the rubber band on her ponytail nice and tight. She didn't warm up or anything. Just looked up at the guy behind the counter and held out her right hand, palm up. Asking for a ball.

He handed her one. She stepped back a few paces, making

the throw about a yard longer. But that was so she could step into her throw.

She took a deep breath and exhaled slowly, smiling to herself. *I got this.*

Even though it *was* a regulation ball, it felt good in her hand. She and her dad always used a regulation ball in the backyard, and she loved the feel of the laces beneath her fingers.

Eye on the hole, she stepped into the throw.

Fired a perfect spiral right through it.

If it had been a basketball shot, the announcers would have said it hit nothin' but net.

The guy bent at the waist, hands on his knees. "Are you kidding?"

"My football girl," Jack Carlisle said to him, proudly slapping a hand onto Alex's shoulder.

Alex had shocked even herself. She hadn't expected the ball to go through, but it had. And maybe she could even do it again. Turning to the man in the booth, she put out her hand and said, "Another ball, please."

"You already won the prize," he said, incredulous.

"Yeah, but my dad paid for three throws," she said. "Gotta get our money's worth."

He handed her another ball, shaking his head. She took an extra step back this time.

The ball whistled through the hole again.

"Show-off," her dad said.

"How old are you?" the guy asked.

"Twelve," Alex replied.

"No way."

"Way," she said.

She put out her hand once more, and he tossed her the last ball. She fired another spiral right through the opening.

"Money," Jack Carlisle said.

"Not for me today," the man said in disappointment. He pointed toward the stuffed animals. "Which one do you want?"

Alex pointed to Simba. The guy used a grabbing stick to lower Simba off the wall of prizes and held it out to Alex. She received it as if he were handing her the Super Bowl trophy.

"You've got some arm for a girl," the young man said.

"I've got some arm, period," she said.

When they got home that night, Alex told her dad what she'd been keeping inside all summer: she wanted to try out for the football team at Orville Middle.

THE WALLS OF ALEX'S ROOM WERE COVERED IN STEELERS POSTERS, and the shelves were lined with soccer and softball trophies and medals. Simba was propped up next to Alex on her bed, taking up about half the mattress and forcing her to relocate some of her smaller stuffed animals to her desk chair.

Alex was prepared for the conversation she and her dad were about to have. She knew trying out for the football team would come with questions and concerns. They'd talked a little about it over dinner, but they continued it here, in her room, surrounded by the greatest football team ever to exist.

It was just the two of them, as always. Alex's mom was living in San Francisco. But she and her mom had a good relationship, even long distance. Her mom now had a four-year-old son with her new husband, Richard.

She got the boy, Alex had thought more than once.

Alex had expected her dad to try to talk her out of it. But he hadn't. He hadn't given his permission yet, either.

"You know why I felt so good today making those throws at the fair?" she said. "Because for a few minutes, I felt like I was in the game."

Her dad was sitting at the end of her bed, facing her.

"I always knew how well you could throw," he said.

"For a girl?" Alex said with a smirk.

"You know me better than that," he said. "And no one knows better than I do how football is your thing."

"But I don't just want it to be a thing when I'm sitting with you at Heinz Field, Dad," she said. "Or next to you on the couch."

"A lot of people love football," he said. "And hardly any of them ever suit up and play."

"Is this about how I might get hurt?"

"Hey," he said. "I know you can get hurt playing any sport. You get tackled in soccer, too, and the only padding you wear is below your knees."

"I hate when they get tackled in the World Cup and beg for calls," Alex said. "I never did that."

"My girl," he said.

He called her that a lot, but this time it made Alex think of something.

"We wouldn't even still be talking about this if I were a boy," she said.

"Hey, you know that's not true," he said. "I have lots of friends who don't want their sons to play. They've all read the news that's come out about concussions and head injuries and all the rest of it."

"But most of those boys will get to play," Alex said. "And there's nothing in the rules that says I can't, if I'm good enough."

"You're right about that," he said. "I checked online while you were setting up for dinner. The announcement on the school website said that the tryouts are open to anybody in the seventh grade." He grinned at her, the fun in his eyes this time.

"Which would include a girl, even if she is most definitely *not* just anybody."

"So I can go for it?" Alex said.

Jack Carlisle breathed a deep sigh. "You can go for it, kiddo."

Alex tackled her dad with a hug, nearly knocking the wind out of him.

"Whoa there—save that energy for the field!" he said.

"The tryouts are next week, though," Alex said, a frown shadowing her face. "The same nights as soccer tryouts."

"Your soccer coach isn't going to be happy," her dad said.

"She's probably not going to be the only one."

Alex's dad stood up and kissed the top of her head before walking toward the bedroom door. He could see how excited and happy she was.

"I love you," Alex said.

"Always nice to hear," he said. "But what did I do in particular?"

"You didn't say no."

"You're the one who's going to be putting herself out there," he said. "How could I possibly say no to something I've been telling you to do your whole life?"

"You think Mom will approve?"

He paused in the doorway. "You don't need her approval," he said. Not in a rude way, just as a matter of fact. "But, yeah, I think she will. You know how big she is on chasing after what you want."

They both knew what he meant. Liza Carlisle—now Dr. Liza Borelli—had wanted to be a doctor more than anything. But she didn't go to med school after college. Instead, she followed her heart and married Alex's dad, and they had Alex a few years later. Suddenly, her dreams of becoming a surgeon began drifting further away from reality. In the end, she had to choose: sacrificing the dream for the family or the family for the dream.

At thirty, she did eventually attend med school, and she and Alex's dad got a divorce. Alex had been four. She didn't understand why her mom was leaving her, no matter how many times either parent tried to explain it. All Alex thought at the time was that her mom didn't want her.

"Someday you'll understand," her mom had said to Alex a few years back.

"You mean how selfish you are?" Alex had replied.

Her dad always said she was old, even when she was young.

"You will always be a big part of my life," her mom said. "But I want more out of my own life than I have, and if I don't do this now, I never will."

Some of Alex's earliest memories were of the day her mother left. She could only remember small things. The suitcases in the front hall. The car waiting to take her mother to the airport. How she couldn't stop crying.

"Dreams and choices are complicated," her mom had said. "Sometimes more complicated for women than men. When you're older, you *will* understand."

And, over time, Alex did. She understood why her mom had chosen to leave, and why it had to happen when it did.

Mostly she understood the part about the complicated nature of dreams.

And choices.

Her mom had made a big one, leaving Alex. Deciding to pursue the career rather than care for her only child. Running away from her obligations, as Alex saw it. And maybe, to an extent, she still felt that way. The feeling of being rejected. It was why, even now, she had difficulty making friends. Really close friends. She had spent a lot of her life being afraid to put herself out there. She wasn't an outcast, exactly. But sometimes she just felt safer being part of the crowd, having a lot of good friends instead of one or two really close ones.

That way she didn't have to risk getting hurt.

But somehow going out for football felt different. Or maybe it was just a different Alex. Like they said on those TV commercials: a new and improved Alex Carlisle.

Even though she hadn't raised the subject with her dad until today, or with any of her friends yet, she had been thinking about trying out for football all summer. And the more she thought about it, the less afraid she became.

She was going for it. Just like her mom. It made her a little proud. Made her feel brave.

Opening up her laptop on her bed, she typed in the school's website and reread the page about tryouts. They'd be spread out over four nights and include skill training, sprints, and a mile run, plus an obstacle course. Alex had never gone through anything this intensive for softball or soccer. But if there was one thing she knew, it was that she could run all day without getting tired.

And there was one other big thing:

She knew she could throw a football as well as anyone her age in Orville, Pennsylvania.

Getting up to look in her closet now, she picked her football off the floor and put her fingers over the laces. The laces felt as good as they had at the fair.

Seeing her hand on the ball brought a smile to her face.

No way the football cared whether a boy or girl was throwing it, she thought.

The door to her room was closed. She was alone with the ball and all her big ideas about making the team.

"Let's do this," she said softly to herself. *"Let's do this."*

Then she stood tall, left hand out in front of her, the ball set over her right shoulder, as if standing in the pocket.

3

ALEX'S DAD WAS LATE GETTING HOME FROM THE OFFICE ON FRIDAY, the night of the football tryouts meeting. The women's intramural basketball league had reserved the middle school gym for that night, so their meeting would take place at Orville High. Alex didn't mind. She liked getting a preview of the hallways she'd be walking through in just a few years. Their neighbor, Kelly, who looked after Alex during the week, offered to drop her off at the high school.

But Alex wanted her dad with her. Not because she was feeling anxious. Just in case she started to.

"This feels a little like my first day of school," Alex said in the car.

"You got this," he said. "And I've got you. Remember that."

The parents were seated in bleachers on both sides of the gym. There was a long table set up underneath the scoreboard. As Alex and her dad entered, some of the teachers from Orville Middle were handing out sign-up forms.

One of them was Mr. Maybin, who'd taught Alex sixth-grade math.

"Hey you," he said to Alex. "What are you doing here?"

"Signing up," Alex said.

"This is for football," Mr. Maybin said, as if Alex had stumbled into the wrong gym.

"I know," Alex said, feeling confident.

"Well, okay then!" he said, a little awkwardly, handing her a form. "Make sure to get a parent or guardian's signature before submitting."

Alex smiled and took the form. "Thanks, Mr. M."

She knew she was going to be the only girl on the gym floor that night. But if she was being honest, she'd known that well before leaving home. Knew from the moment she'd decided to try out. But now she was here. No turning back. There were seventh-grade boys seated on both sides of the basketball court, with a wide lane cutting between. Alex walked up that lane now, feeling every eye in the gym on her. Some of them even belonged to the parents up in the bleachers with her dad. She heard some giggles, too. And some whispers. But then relief washed over her when she spotted a familiar face in the crowd—tan, freckled cheeks, a messy crop of chestnut brown curls, skinny legs crossed in front of him. She'd gone to school with Gabe Hildreth since kindergarten, and they shared all the same classes. Over the years, they'd grown to be pretty good friends. Gabe had been a star wide receiver on the sixth-grade team at Orville Middle.

Alex walked over to where he was sitting, and he made some room. She sat down next to him.

Now Gabe was whispering.

"What are you doing here?" he said.

"What you're doing here," she whispered back. "Trying out for football."

The coach of this year's seventh-grade team was a man named Ed Mencken, a phys ed teacher at the high school who Alex knew had played football with her dad when they went to Orville High. Mr. Mencken had been a tight end, according to Alex's dad. Alex spotted him now up near the table and thought he looked to be in good enough shape to go out for a pass right now.

But he wasn't going out for any passes at the moment. He was walking down the aisle between his prospective players, straight in Alex's direction.

"Excuse me, young lady," he said.

"Yes, sir?" she said.

He was standing over her now.

"Are you in the right place?" Mr. Mencken asked, totally serious.

"Yes, sir," Alex said. But the way he said it made her feel a little unsure herself.

If everybody in the gym hadn't been staring at her before, they were now. Mr. Mencken had a voice as big as himself.

"This meeting is about football tryouts," he said, as if Alex were a confused child lost in the woods.

Alex's dad was in the front row of the bleachers, to her right. He could hear what Mr. Mencken had said. Alex was pretty sure the whole gym heard. Her dad stood now, and Alex held her breath, worried he might make this moment even more awkward for her than it already was.

"She's in the right place, Ed," he said.

Mr. Mencken turned to see where the voice was coming from. Then he saw who it belonged to.

"Your daughter?" he said to Jack Carlisle.

Alex's dad gave a quick nod. "Yes, sir."

Mr. Mencken looked as if he wanted to say something more

but decided against it. He simply walked back to the table, picked up the microphone (even though Alex couldn't imagine why he needed one), and started talking about this year's team.

He said that of all the boys in the gym, twenty-four of them would make the team. That's how he said it: boys. As if he'd forgotten Alex was there. Or maybe he was ignoring her. He said the Owls would play an eight-game schedule against other middle schools in their area, and at the end of the season there would be a championship game between the two teams with the best records. The game would be played the Saturday before Thanksgiving.

Then he described what they should expect over the four nights of tryouts.

"From now on, I'll be Coach Mencken," he said. "Even though we haven't picked the team yet, the season starts Monday night. This will be a real training camp, not some summer camp. You boys—" This time he managed to stop himself. "You *all* are going to work harder over the next few days than you've ever worked on anything in your lives."

He smiled, but didn't look all that happy to Alex.

"And you're going to love it," he said with a smirk.

He walked back up to the table and turned around, facing everybody in the gym at once.

"And if you're not willing to put in the work to be the best football player you can be, then don't bother filling out that form in your hand," he said. "Because this isn't the team for you and I'm not the coach for you."

From somewhere behind Alex she heard someone say, "I heard this guy was tough."

If Mr. Mencken heard, he didn't let on.

"Long story short?" he said. "I'm a football guy. And I want football guys playing for me."

Alex swore he was looking at her again as he said that. Or maybe she'd just imagined it.

I'm as much a football guy as anybody in the gym, she thought.

Coach Mencken put down the microphone. The meeting was over. But a lot of the boys from her school were still staring daggers at Alex.

"You never said anything about wanting to play football," Gabe said when they were standing. The parents were up and chatting now, some asking Coach Mencken questions about the team. The other seventh graders were milling about, catching up on their summers.

"I didn't make up my mind to try out until the last couple of days," she said, then shrugged. "And then I figured if I told you, you'd only try to talk me out of it. So I decided to surprise you . . . and I guess everybody else."

He blew out some air. But he was smiling.

"Well," he said, "mission accomplished on that."

"Mr. Mencken didn't seem too happy to see me," Alex said.

"From what I hear," Gabe said, "the only thing that makes him happy is winning football games."

"Maybe he'll like the idea of a girl on his team better if I show him I can do that," she said, then paused. "How do you feel about all this?"

She didn't clarify, but knew Gabe understood what she meant. How did he feel about her trying out for the team?

"Doesn't matter," he said.

"It does to me."

"I just don't want you to get hurt," Gabe said.

"Anybody can get hurt playing football," Alex said.

Gabe gave her a long look and said, "I wasn't just talking about getting hurt on the field."

Alex knew he spoke the truth. Already she could tell that Coach was skeptical of her. What would the rest of the guys think? But she couldn't worry about that now. Today was a win.

"See you Monday night," Alex said before catching up with her dad.

"Unless you change your mind, of course," Gabe said.

"I won't," she said. "Come on. You know me better than that."

"Yeah," he said. "I do."

"You always knew I loved football . . ." she said.

"I thought that meant *watching* it."

"Maybe I finally got tired of just watching."

Gabe walked toward his dad then, and Alex looked around for hers. She saw him underneath one of the side baskets, talking to Mr. Mencken. Her dad seemed to be doing most of the talking. But at least he appeared to be acting cordial.

When they were in the car Alex asked, "What was that all about with Coach?"

"I just wanted to make sure we understood each other."

"*Dad*," she said. "What did you say to him?"

"I told him I wanted him to treat you the same as every other player on that field and work you just as hard."

"And that was it?"

"Pretty much . . ."

"*Daaaad*," she said.

She could see a smile creep onto his face.

"I might have mentioned one other thing."

Now he was really smiling.

"What?" she said.

"I might have told him that if he tried to work you harder than everybody else, or didn't give you a fair shot at making the team, I'd tell everybody that he used to cry like a little baby when we lost a game."

"He did?" Alex said. "For real?"

"Waa waa waa," her dad said, mimicking a whining toddler.

"Wait," Alex said. "There's no crying in baseball, but I never heard about football . . ."

One of their favorite movies to watch together was *A League of Their Own*, about the All-American Girls Professional Baseball League. Alex's favorite moment was when the team manager, played by Tom Hanks, told one of his players, "There's no crying in baseball."

"Same rule applies," her dad said, winking.

COACH HAD SENT OUT AN EMAIL BLAST OVER THE WEEKEND TO ALL who had registered for tryouts, explaining how there would be no contact or tackling drills until the roster had been set. The team's first official practice would be held the following week, at the start of the school year.

But he reminded all the players who'd be attending the tryouts to show up on Monday night with helmets and shoulder pads.

The last line of the email read: "There will still be football activities this week. You all need to get used to dressing like football players."

Alex didn't have a helmet or pads. There had never been any reason for her to have them.

Until now.

On Sunday afternoon, Alex and her dad went shopping at the Dick's Sporting Goods in downtown Orville. By then Jack Carlisle had done some online research about the best and safest helmets for twelve-year-old players. He told Alex it was the first time he'd had to think about buying a helmet since he was in high school and his own father had taken him to the local sporting goods store, back before superstores like Dick's existed.

"Gotta tell you, kiddo," he said. "These things cost a lot more than they did when I was playing."

Alex grinned.

"I'll bet a loaf of bread does, too," she said.

"And I can't believe how many different kinds there are," he said.

"Waa waa waa," she said, leaning into her dad.

All joking aside, Alex knew how lucky she was to have a dad like hers. One who not only supported her dreams but helped her reach them. She never took that for granted.

The manager of Dick's, Mr. Pritchett, was an old friend of Alex's dad. Over the years, they had bought Alex's softball glove and bat and soccer shin pads and soccer spikes at Dick's.

This trip to the store was different.

When Mr. Pritchett greeted them, he said to Alex, "Don't tell me. You grew out of last year's soccer cleats, right?"

"We're actually looking for a football helmet," her dad said.

Mr. Pritchett looked genuinely confused.

"Who for?" he said.

"Alex," Jack Carlisle said, like it should be obvious.

Mr. Pritchett looked down at Alex. She smiled at him and shrugged. Then he looked over at her dad.

"Seriously?" he said.

"We hardly ever joke about football at our house," Alex's dad said.

"She's going out for the team?" Mr. Pritchett said.

"That she is." He put one arm around Alex and squeezed tight. Almost like he knew what was coming and was bracing Alex for it.

"But, uh . . . are you sure she can, um . . ." Mr. Pritchett paused, as if the rest of his thought had gotten stuck in his throat somewhere.

"Try out? Handle the pressure? Make the team?" Alex's dad guessed, knowing full well that wasn't what Mr. Pritchett was asking. "We wouldn't be here if the answer to any of those questions was no."

"I've sold girls lacrosse helmets before," Mr. Pritchett said. "But I don't believe I've ever sold a football helmet to a girl."

Alex thought he made it sound as if he were about to sell a bicycle to a fish.

"Well, Scott, my old friend," Alex's dad said, clapping him on the back, "there's a first time for everything, isn't there?"

Then he told Mr. Pritchett that he was actually looking for a specific helmet, one he'd researched, a Riddell Youth Speed Flex.

"They're kind of expensive," Mr. Pritchett said.

"And kind of safe, too, from what I read," Alex's dad said.

Mr. Pritchett chuckled. "Helmets were a lot cheaper in our day."

"So was a loaf of bread," Jack Carlisle said.

He gave Alex a quick wink. She winked back. They were sharing a private joke.

Even though football, more than ever, was no joke with them.

The colors for the Orville High team were blue and white, and the helmets were white with blue trim. The kids trying out for the seventh-grade team were encouraged to buy white helmets, too, if possible. Coach Mencken made some suggestions about brands in his email but said parents were free to buy whatever they thought was safest.

Alex's dad told her that the Speed Flex had gotten a five-star rating on safety and comfort.

"I was looking for six stars out of five, to tell you the truth," he'd said to Alex on the way to the store. "I've read the same stuff about concussions as everybody else."

"I know this isn't easy for you, Dad," Alex had said. "But I appreciate you letting me do it anyway."

Mr. Pritchett said they were in luck. He'd just gotten a shipment of Riddell youth helmets that included the Speed Flex. And in the Orville blue and white.

"What am I gonna stock?" he said to Alex's dad. "Notre Dame colors?"

Once Alex had a Speed Flex on her head, she thought it was pretty much the coolest thing she'd ever worn in her life. There were inflatable pockets on the inside that were supposed to provide extra protection. Alex had done some research of her own. The consensus seemed to be that the helmet should fit without having to fasten the chin straps. Hers did. But fastening the straps turned out to be no problem.

She secured the chin straps in place and walked over to look at herself in a mirror.

"It's perfect," she said to her dad.

"But does it really fit?"

"It fits so well that I may sleep in it," she said.

"Okay, that's weird."

She took off the helmet and carried it with her to the section where the shoulder pads were. Dick's carried three different brands, the names of which they recognized from the research they'd done. But they were set on Wilson Rush pads, which provided the same support as the other brands but just looked a little sleeker to Alex, even though no one except her was ever going to see them once she had her jersey on.

If she got to wear a blue Orville jersey.

When she looked at herself in the mirror with the pads on over her T-shirt, she thought she looked a little bit like Iron Man.

"I look like I'm on my way to Avengers practice," she said to her dad.

"Maybe you should be, instead of football practice," Alex heard from behind her.

Jeff Stiles, who'd been the quarterback on the sixth-grade team, and his dad had come walking into the shoulder pad section of Dick's.

"What did you say?" Alex said to Jeff.

Jeff tried to act surprised. "Hey, Alex," he said. "I didn't say anything."

But she knew what she'd heard, whether he wanted to admit it or not.

"Hey, Jeff," she said. "You're gearing up, too, I guess?"

"Just some new pads," he said. "I've got my same helmet from last season."

"Like he's going to have the same job," Mr. Stiles said, putting his arm around his son's shoulders. "QB 1."

Starting quarterback. His dad made it sound as if Jeff getting the job were a foregone conclusion.

Jeff looked at Alex.

"So you're still doing this, huh?"

"I must be," Alex said. "I think these pads would look pretty silly at soccer practice."

"A lot of the guys think it's pretty silly for a girl to try out for our team," came Jeff's retort.

"And not just the boys on the team," Mr. Stiles added.

Jack Carlisle smiled at Jeff's dad. But Alex knew her dad. It was the fakest one he had.

"You mean the parents, Bob?" Jack Carlisle said. "Last time I checked, middle school sports were supposed to be about the kids."

"Like girls go out for football teams all the time," Mr. Stiles said with an arrogant laugh.

"Not all the time," Alex's dad said. "Just this time. And like it's always been: the ones who are good enough are the ones who get the jobs, same as it was when you and I were getting after it in high school."

Alex looked to see what Mr. Stiles's reaction would be. Her dad had told her that when he and Mr. Stiles were at Orville High, they'd both gone out for quarterback. Jack Carlisle had won the position as a sophomore and had kept it all the way through their senior season. Mr. Stiles had been a running back.

"Yeah," Mr. Stiles said. He didn't even try to hide the sarcasm in his voice. "Good times."

"Well, see you tomorrow night," Alex said to Jeff.

"Good times," he said, rolling his eyes.

There was one more thing for them to buy before football tryouts the following night:

A football.

Alex would have been fine if seventh graders used a regulation-size ball. She already knew she could grip one just fine. After all, she'd thrown a regulation ball at the fair to win Simba. But by now, she'd discovered they would be using an intermediate-size ball, a Youth Size 7.

A regulation ball, the size they used for high school football and college and the pros, was a 9.

Alex's dad bought her a Youth 7 to take home with them, along with her new helmet and Iron Man pads.

The second they were home, Alex hurried to put on her helmet and pads, so she and her dad could practice with the new ball in the backyard.

"Did you hear what Jeff said?" Alex said to her dad.

"I did," he said. "And I heard what his dad said, plain as day. Apparently he's convinced that the football gods want his son to be the quarterback he never was."

He shook his head. "It's just football," he continued. "But some things never change, even from when I was a kid. Some of the parents in the gym the other night were still making it out to be more serious than climate change."

"I take it seriously," Alex said.

"That's different," he said.

"How?"

"Because this is your dream," he said. "And you're allowed to chase your own dreams as hard as you can."

"I do want this, Dad," she said. "And I'm not gonna lie: Jeff and his dad's attitude today made me want it even more."

"It's not about them," her dad said in a stern voice. "It's about you."

"I know."

"And yes, I know how much you want this, sweetheart," he said.

She knew there was no way in the world he could see her smiling at him from behind her facemask.

"I'd appreciate it," she said, "if you wouldn't call me sweetheart when I'm in uniform."

"Consider it done," he said.

He jogged out to the middle of their yard. She threw him a pass, and then another, and another. Every time she caught the ball, she'd rub it up a little, like a pitcher with a new baseball, trying to bang it up a little. Make it feel less slick. She'd read about how when NFL teams got a new shipment of footballs, they'd do all sorts of crazy things to break them in for their quarterbacks, including sticking them inside a sack and banging it against a wall.

But the laces felt the same to her. And she felt as if she could control the smaller ball even better than a 9.

"How's it feeling?" her dad asked, starting to back up a little.

"Sweet," she said.

"Please don't say 'sweet' when you're in uniform, sweetheart," he said.

Everything was fine back here, Alex thought, just the two of them. Like always. Playing a game of catch. Alex knew it wasn't going to be anything like this tomorrow. She was going to feel like the new kid at school, even though she'd known most of these boys from growing up in Orville. She had lived here her whole life. But tomorrow she would feel like an outsider.

The girl who was always holding back, now putting herself out there, knowing that just about every other kid on the field had already made up their mind about her. Rejection was a feeling Alex knew well. Didn't make it any less painful, though.

She had heard it in Jeff Stiles's voice today. And he didn't even know her dream. At least not all of it.

"You can really catch the ball," her dad said. "Coach might take a look at those hands and try to turn you into a wide receiver."

Alex had the ball. She didn't respond, just motioned with her left hand for her dad to go long, toward their deer fencing at the end of the yard.

She let the ball go, not putting too much air underneath it, not wanting her dad to be too close to the fence when he caught up with her pass.

He wasn't. He reached up and caught the spiral with plenty of room to spare.

"I'm not a wide receiver," Alex said, taking off her helmet and shaking out her long brown hair. "I'm a quarterback."

BUT WAS SHE, REALLY?

Was she good enough to play quarterback?

Why? Because she could hit her dad with passes in the back-yard when nobody was watching? Because she had enough arm and accuracy to win a stuffed animal at the town fair?

Alex was alone in her room. She'd set her helmet and pads on the rocking chair in the corner and spread out on her bed, new football clutched under her arm, laptop open across her lap. Her dad was downstairs watching the Pirates game on TV.

She was up here. Alone with her questions.

And her doubts.

It had all been so exciting at first, making the decision to try out. But then she'd gone to the meeting and seen the reaction all around her in that gym—from the boys, from the coach, and probably from just about every parent there except her own father.

Her dad had always told her she could do anything she set her mind to if she was willing to put in the work. And if she was good enough. And that didn't just apply to sports.

That's how Alex wanted this to go, hoped it would go.

Dreamed it would go.

She would show them she was good enough, and they would let her play, even if it meant playing quarterback.

But would it go that way?

Would Coach Mencken *be* that way?

Even Gabe, one of her best friends at school, didn't seem all that thrilled about her showing up at the gym. Alex was worried that he might get some heat from the other guys if he showed support for her. Probably more if he embraced her as a teammate.

Maybe she'd even lose him as a friend.

She still hadn't talked about the tryouts with any of her other friends, even though they all probably knew by now. Alex had purposely avoided Instagram since she'd gone to the meeting. Word traveled fast in a small town like Orville, and there were at least fifty guys her age at the meeting. Everybody in the grade had to be talking about it. None of her soccer teammates had reached out to her, but *they* had to be talking about it, too. The thought made Alex's stomach turn. Trying out for football meant she couldn't play soccer this season. The girls would be livid when they found out.

Or maybe it wasn't nearly as big a deal as she was making it out to be.

It's a big deal to me, Alex thought.

She wasn't even completely sure why it was, though. Why this had become such a runaway dream so quickly. But it had. Maybe it was because she hadn't pushed herself enough. Maybe it was because there was a part of her always feeling as if she were holding herself back.

Or possibly it was just as her mom had told her all those years ago, and Alex would have to be older before she understood.

All she knew for now, no matter how many questions and

doubts she had, was that she was going to be on that field tomorrow night, in helmet and pads.

Not trying to be a superhero.

Just there to show them that she belonged, whether they wanted her there or not.

There was an old Dr. Seuss book Alex loved when she was little called *Oh, the Places You'll Go!* Her mom used to read it to her at night before bed. It was maybe the thing she remembered best about the time before her mom left. When she was still in the house, and really in Alex's life.

She could hear her mom's voice inside her head right now, telling her that today was her day, that she was off to great places.

Off and away.

Not today, Alex told herself in her room.

Tomorrow.

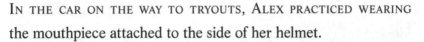

In the car on the way to tryouts, Alex practiced wearing the mouthpiece attached to the side of her helmet.

She had never worn a mouthpiece before. She asked her dad if it was absolutely necessary that she wear one on the field tonight. He insisted that it was.

"But I have a facemask," she argued.

"You've mentioned that already," he said.

"Isn't a facemask supposed to protect, well, your *face*? Which includes your mouth?"

He smiled at her, then lightly tapped one of his front teeth with his index finger.

"Fake," he said. "And I wore a facemask, too."

"Oh," she said.

"Oh indeed," he said. "I'd prefer if my football girl didn't end up with a hockey player's smile."

They were in the parking lot outside the football field at Orville High. Since Coach Mencken taught at the high school, and was there during the day for Teacher Planning week, it was easier for the players to meet him on campus for tryouts. Jack Carlisle had come home from work early so he could take Alex to the five o'clock tryouts. Alex told him he didn't have to stay.

"Like I'm going to miss this," he said.

"I've been thinking . . ." she said.

"Don't overdo the thinking," he said. "You're going to be great."

"I've mostly been thinking that just because I think I'm good enough doesn't mean I *am* good enough."

"Attitude," her dad said.

"But what if I mess up?" she said. "The boys will never let me forget it. By the time I get home tonight, I might be the laughing-stock of Orville Middle before school even starts."

He made a snorting noise.

"Anything but that!" he said. "Do you think you might go viral, too?"

"I'm serious."

"So am I," he said. "You're not here for them. You're here for you, and to prove something to yourself. If you start feeling a little wobbly out there, I'll be up in the stands. You just look for me."

"You might be the only one rooting for me," she said.

"Only one you need, pumpkin pie."

He pulled her close to him, smiling at her, showing her all his teeth, including one that she hadn't ever known was fake. Then he kissed her squarely on the facemask.

"Never kissed a quarterback before," Jack Carlisle said to his daughter.

7

ALEX ONLY THOUGHT SHE WAS EARLY.

When she walked out onto the field, though, a lot of boys were already out there warming up. She saw that none of them were wearing their helmets and quickly took off hers. She didn't want to do anything to attract attention, at least until she got her chance to show them her stuff.

She looked around for Gabe but couldn't spot him. Jeff Stiles was on the other side of the field, soft-tossing to Lewis Healey. She knew from Gabe that Lewis had been one of the other wide receivers on the sixth-grade team last year. Alex could see why. He seemed to be the tallest boy out here.

A big target, Alex thought, then smiled to herself.

Already thinking like a quarterback.

Alex watched Jeff throw. He was just warming up, so there was no need to be airing it out yet. But he didn't appear to Alex like a natural-born QB. From the time Alex had started throwing with her dad, long before there was even the seed of an idea about playing football, he had talked about how natural her over-the-top motion was.

Jeff Stiles didn't have that kind of motion. He seemed to drop down when he threw. Not sidearm, exactly. More three-quarters. It was the way NFL quarterbacks threw the ball around pass rushers. Only Jeff wasn't being rushed.

But this was the guy who was supposed to be QB 1 just by showing up.

Alex stood by herself, trying to decide if she should join a group on the field, when she felt a tap on her shoulder. She turned and saw it was Gabe. Jabril Wise was with him. Alex remembered him from the couple of games she'd watched of the sixth-grade team last season. Jabril had played middle linebacker then and was likely going to be the middle linebacker now. When Alex had watched him play, Jabril had seemed to be everywhere on the field at once, whether sacking the quarterback, bringing down ball carriers in the open field, or knocking the ball away from a receiver when he'd drop back into coverage. She'd left the game thinking that the Steelers could use him.

From what she'd heard about Jabril from Gabe, Alex knew she was going to like him a lot. For one, he was smiling at her now, which was more than she could say for the rest of the guys. He was about Alex's height, with a lean, athletic build. He wore his black hair in tight cornrows against his dark brown skin.

"You owe me a dollar," Jabril said to Alex now.

"How do you figure?"

"I bet Gabe a dollar you wouldn't show," he said. "Since it's technically your fault, I figure you're on the hook for it."

Alex grinned. Then she turned to look at Gabe.

"So you bet that I *would* show?"

"I never bet on anything unless I know I'll win," Gabe said. "And I know how stubborn you are."

"But that's a good thing in football, right?" Alex said.

Gabe grinned and shook his head, putting a fist out. Alex

bumped it with her own. Across the field, she could see that Jeff had stopped throwing to stare at them.

"We're gonna find out how good it is," Gabe said.

"Be honest, how many guys on this field want me here?" Alex said.

Gabe looked at Jabril. "You wanna take this one?"

Jabril bristled. "Other than us, you mean?" he said. "Nobody."

"Why not you guys?" Alex asked.

"Me and Gabe?" Jabril said. "We're as stubborn as you are. Plus, we're your friends."

Alex's face lit up. She pretty much just met this guy, and already he'd called himself her friend without a second thought. If only the other guys would be as welcoming . . .

A few minutes later, Coach Mencken called them all to the middle of the field. He kept his opening comments brief, reminding them again how many of the players on the field would actually make the team. He said that it wasn't just some number he'd pulled out of thin air; it was a league rule.

"Two dozen make it," he said. "By my count, there are four dozen of you on this field. I'm just gonna assume that everybody here doesn't want to be in the half that doesn't make my team."

His team, Alex thought.

He clapped his hands. It sounded as loud as thunder to Alex.

"Now let's start finding out who *is* going to make my team."

Mr. Wise, Jabril's dad, was one of the parents helping evaluate players as they went through their drills. Alex's heart sank a little as she realized Mr. Stiles was the other. But because Jeff was trying out for offense and Jabril was trying out for defense,

Mr. Stiles would be grading the defensive players and Mr. Wise would do the same with the guys going through the offensive drills.

Mr. Wise knew what to look for in offensive players because he'd played two years in the NFL as a linebacker with the Jets before a knee injury ended his career. Jabril had told her this earlier.

"Y'all better be ready to work," Mr. Wise said as he ushered the offensive players to the far end of the field, Alex among them.

He worked them hard. Coach Mencken would watch for a few minutes, then head to the other end of the field to watch the defense. Both Mr. Wise and Mr. Stiles were carrying clipboards and would occasionally scribble down a note or two.

At first everybody, both ends of the field, was doing ladder drills, to show off their footwork. Rope ladders were laid out in the grass, and players had to make their way through them in various ways, as fast as they could. Sometimes they high-stepped right through the spaces. Other times they had to step in the spaces using only their left foot, with their right foot outside, almost like hopscotch.

Then they ran what Coach Mencken called "gassers." They all lined up on the goal line. Ran to the ten-yard line. Touched the ground. Back to the goal line. Then to the fifteen-yard line. Touched the ground there. Came back. Then to the twenty.

"Now I know why they call these gassers," Lewis Healey said. "I'm already running out of gas."

Alex was tired after they finished. But not gassed. She had always been able to run all day in soccer. Now she was just doing it in helmet and pads.

They took a water break after the gasser drill. Then Mr. Wise laid down two rope ladders side by side. He said two players at a time would race each other. Up and back.

"Might as well start competing now," he said.

When it was Alex's turn, she was set to race Lewis Healey.

Mr. Wise would blow the whistle when it was time for them to start.

Alex took her stance.

The whistle blew.

But as Alex took off, she felt a foot on her heel from behind and lost her balance. She fell facedown, five feet before she even got to the ladder. Behind her, she heard an eruption of laughter. But she scrambled to her feet, determined to finish even though there was no chance of beating Lewis.

When Alex finally did finish, she saw that Jeff Stiles had been behind her in line. He flashed her a smug grin. She wanted to say something, but there was just no point. He would never admit that he'd tripped her. If any of the other players had seen, they might even be happy he'd done it.

"Looks like you got brought down from behind by an imaginary tackler," Jeff said. He slapped a low five to the guy behind him in line as they laughed.

Jeff was getting ready to race Gabe. Alex just kept walking. But she looked up in the stands to where she knew her father was. She caught his eye. He just nodded. Alex wondered if he knew what had happened.

She did.

• • •

It wasn't until the end of the ninety minutes that Coach Mencken, working with the offense now, said they were going to do some throwing and catching in the time they had left. When he asked who his quarterbacks were, only one player raised his hand:

Jeff Stiles.

Until Alex raised *her* hand.

"Really?" Jeff snorted. "You think you're quarterback material?"

"Unless I trip myself up," Alex said, alluding to the stunt he pulled back at the ladders.

"You really want to try out for quarterback, Miss Carlisle?" Coach Mencken said.

"Yes, sir," she affirmed.

"Is it because your dad was a quarterback?" Coach said.

"No, sir." She took a deep breath, let it out. "It's because I think I can be one."

Coach grimaced. "Aren't you worried about getting hurt back there in the pocket?"

"Pretty sure anybody can get hurt standing in a pocket, Coach," Alex said. "Unless they're quick enough to avoid the rush."

Alex didn't feel as if she were talking back to him or being fresh. He'd asked her a question. She'd given him an honest answer. He looked as if he wanted to say something more but stopped himself. He might not want a girl on his team. But he had to know that anything he said in front of her and the other players would be the same as saying it in front of her dad.

All he said was this: "We've got about fifteen minutes. Jeff, you throw first."

Before long, Alex got the idea that Jeff was going to be the only one doing any throwing tonight. Receivers lined up to his right and left. They ran ten-yard patterns, making inside cuts and then cuts to the outside. It was clear to Alex—clear as day, as her dad liked to say—that even though Lewis was taller, Gabe was the best of all of them. He made the cleanest cuts. You could see he had the surest hands, able to adjust even if the throw wasn't perfect.

And not many of the throws were perfect. Far from it.

Jeff Stiles *didn't* have a great arm, or a particularly accurate one.

It was a good arm. He wasn't wild or anything like that. But Alex's dad said you knew a really good thrower when you saw one. Alex didn't think she was seeing one in Jeff, even if he acted as if the quarterback job was already his.

But he kept throwing. Alex imagined a scoreboard clock inside her head, with time winding down, wondering if she would even get the chance to show off her arm before it was time to go home.

Finally Coach told Gabe to go deep.

"Turn it loose," Coach said. "Show me what you got, Jeff."

He's Jeff. *I'm* Miss Carlisle.

Jeff was in the end zone. Gabe was at the twenty when Jeff released the ball. It was high, and short. Gabe slowed down to catch it at the thirty-yard line, making the throw look better than it really was.

"That arm just keeps getting stronger and stronger!" Mr. Stiles yelled from behind Coach's shoulder.

He'd come down from the other end to watch, along with the defensive players.

Coach turned to Alex.

"We've only got a couple of minutes," he said. "Would you rather wait and get some reps tomorrow night?"

"No, sir," she said. "I'd like to get some throws in right now, if that's okay with you."

He paused and surveyed the other players, as if considering what he wanted to do. Maybe he could feel Jack Carlisle's eyes on him now.

"Once through the receivers on both sides," he said. "Then we call it a night."

Her first throw was over the middle to Lewis Healey. The ball felt great coming out of Alex's hand. A tight spiral, just as Lewis made his cut.

But Lewis slowed down the last couple of yards, Alex noticed, even if nobody else could, and the ball sailed past him, out of reach.

"Led me too much," Lewis said as he ran past her, putting his hands out in a helpless gesture.

Alex ignored him and just concentrated on making the rest of her throws. She was nervous, but it didn't show in her execution. She threw one solid pass after another. Her dad had told her to focus only on herself. But it was hard not to measure herself against Jeff. She couldn't remember how many throws Jeff had made. But she'd only gotten to make eight.

It was practically like she hadn't thrown at all.

Coach Mencken blew his whistle and started to walk toward the sidelines, signaling that the workout was over.

"Hey, Coach," Gabe said.

Coach stopped and turned around.

Gabe would tell Alex later on the phone that he was amazed that the words had even made their way out of his mouth.

"What is it, Gabe?" Coach said.

"Alex didn't get to throw a deep ball," he said.

Alex was standing at the goal line, the ball still in her hand. Coach took an impatient look at his watch before glancing back at Gabe.

"One more throw," Coach said. "And then we really are done."

Gabe ran over near the right sideline. He looked at Alex and nodded. Alex knew that every other player on the field was watching them now.

"Post pattern," Alex called to Gabe.

He would take off down the sideline, then break to the middle of the field.

Alex leaned over, as if taking a snap from an imaginary center.

"*Go!*" she yelled.

Gabe sprinted out. Alex took a three-step drop, the one she'd been practicing in the yard with her dad. When she looked up, she saw Gabe making his cut toward the middle, at the twenty-yard line. Where he'd been when Jeff released the ball on his turn.

Alex waited.

If she was going to air it out, she was *really* going to air it out.

Gabe was between the thirty-five-yard line and the forty when Alex's spiral came out of the sky and landed in his hands. For a second Alex thought Gabe might run the rest of the way down the field. But he just turned and came right back.

When he got to Alex, he tossed her the ball.

"Nice throw," he said.

"Thanks."

Coach looked at Alex, then Gabe, then back at Alex.

"You've got some arm," he said.

He didn't call her Miss Carlisle this time.

At the end of the night, Coach announced that they were going to scrimmage on the last day of tryouts. Flags, no tackle. But it would be eleven-on-eleven, offense against defense.

"I want to see you competing against each other," Coach Mencken said.

When he said that Alex thought: *All I've been doing is competing, as hard as I know how.*

Two nights later, her mom called. It was the first time they'd spoken since tryouts had begun, and Alex was sore all over from the grueling drills.

"Are you still good with me doing this?" Alex said.

"One hundred percent," her mom said. "Or a hundred and ten. Isn't that the expression they use in sports? You know this isn't exactly my area of expertise."

"No kidding, Mom," Alex said. "It's like that old coach once said."

"Go ahead."

"You don't know if a football is blown up or stuffed."

Her mom laughed at the other end of the line, from the other side of the country.

"Well," she said, "you got me there."

Alex gave her the rundown of the last few nights. How well she thought she'd thrown, especially compared to Jeff Stiles. She told her how she was sure Jeff had tripped her, and how Lewis intentionally missed a ball to make her look bad. Or maybe to make Jeff look better.

"Welcome to the world, my darling," her mom said. "You're finding out now what most women find out eventually, sometimes the hard way."

"What's that?"

"That being as good as the guys isn't always good enough," she said. "You've got to be better, even when you're going after the same job."

"That doesn't sound fair," Alex said.

"No one said it was fair," her mom said.

Sometimes Alex felt as if she were speaking with an older sister and not her mom.

"Any other words of wisdom?" Alex asked.

"Sure. When they go low, you go high."

"Pretty sure you stole that one from Michelle Obama, Mom," Alex said.

"Doesn't mean it isn't solid advice."

An hour later, Alex was sitting on the back porch with her dad, the two of them listening to the crickets and watching fireflies. Alex once asked her dad what fireflies did during the day. He'd smiled and said sometimes it was more fun to imagine than to know for real.

"What if I don't make it?" she said to her dad now.

"I think you will," he said. "I was there tonight. I was there the other two nights. I've watched both quarterbacks. And I think you're the best one. If this really is an open competition, not only will you make the team, you'll start."

Alex snorted. "Like that's gonna happen," she said.

"Not saying it's gonna happen," her dad said. "Just saying it should."

"Only because you're my dad."

"No, no—I'm serious," he said. "I may be a little biased, but I was a quarterback once, too. And I'd tell you if I thought you weren't the best one out there. If Coach Mencken's going to keep two, you should be one of them."

She looked out into the backyard and imagined the fireflies chasing each other around in the dark.

"And whatever happens, sweetheart, I'm proud of you," he said. "And you should be proud of yourself."

"Still one night to go," she reminded him. "Coach said we're going to scrimmage. I hope I get to take some snaps."

"If I were my old friend Ed," Jack Carlisle said, "I'd want to see what you can do in something even close to a game situation. You've got the arm. And that's something you either have or you don't. Everything else about playing quarterback you can learn on the job. But you can't teach talent."

"Even if you're a girl?" she said.

"I think it's way more impressive because you're a girl. You've got double the pressure."

"I'm just me, Dad," she said.

Jack Carlisle put his arm around his daughter.

"Are you ever," he said.

• • •

Her dad came home early from work the next afternoon. Alex joked that he needed to rest up for all the spectating he'd be doing from the stands during the last night of tryouts.

"It does take a lot out of me," he said. "Not so much the physical exertion. It's the stress of not being able to control what goes on out there."

"Would you rather be down on the field playing?" Alex asked. But she already knew the answer.

He smiled. "Anybody would want to be your age and down on the field playing," he said.

Alex asked him if it was all right if she rode her bike into town. There were still a few hours to kill before the scrimmage, and the downtown area of Orville was only six blocks from their house. Alex actually could have walked to town. She just preferred being on her bike.

She liked going fast, pretending she was flying through an open field.

"Ah. I see. *You're* the one who doesn't want to sit around stressing about practice," he said.

"Is it that obvious?" she said, a bit sheepish.

"As obvious as you needing some soft serve at Bostwick's," he said, handing her some ice cream money. "I'd get sprinkles, too."

"Just to be on the safe side."

She rode up Main Street, past Sam's Pizza and Delvecchio's Market and Taylor Books. She crossed over at the corner of Elm Street and came back down the other side, past the movie theater and the UPS Store and the Party Shoppe and the new Starbucks. She thought about all the times this summer when she'd ridden her bike through the downtown streets of Orville before she decided to try out for the team. It wasn't like she didn't have a care in the world then. More like she was still trying to figure out who she wanted to be.

At that time, her secret desire to play football was still just a thought. Nothing she planned to act on. But soon enough, that desire would turn into a need. And her secret would no longer be a secret.

Alex had a lot of secrets, even from her dad.

He didn't know she'd cried after the first night of tryouts, after Jeff Stiles had tripped her and then Lewis had gone out of his way to make her look bad. It shouldn't have been like that. They were all trying to do the same thing and make the team. And if Alex made the roster, whether they wanted her to or not, they were all going to be on the *same* team. They were going to be teammates. Teammates pulled for each other. Or so she'd always thought.

And if she did make it, did they think Alex was just going to magically forget that they'd intentionally sabotaged her? Maybe they didn't want her to.

What she was doing was hard enough. Couldn't they see that? Why would they try to make it harder? Regardless of all that had happened during tryouts, Alex kept coming back, facing the torment and ridicule day after day, just to make the team. She wasn't afraid.

So why were they?

Alex hated meanness and bullies. She knew that Jeff and Lewis were careful not to make their bullying obvious. But she knew. And she knew *they* knew.

She'd hated that they'd made her cry. But it wasn't just the bullying. It was that she felt so alone in all this. She knew her dad loved and supported her, but he couldn't totally understand what she was going through. Her mom could. But she was all the way on the other side of the country. She didn't want her dad to see her cry. Not only because they'd joked about no crying in football, but also because she thought it would seem to him that football was causing her pain, and not just the physical kind. He'd tell her she could quit. That you shouldn't participate in anything that's making you miserable. But the truth was that it wasn't football making her miserable. Not really.

She'd had the same feeling that first night that she would have all week: of all the guys out there, only Gabe and Jabril seemed to be pulling for her. But what would it be like for them if she did make the team? No doubt they'd be hearing it from their teammates if they sided with Alex.

But aren't we all supposed to be on the same side?

She'd buried her face in her pillow that first night and let the tears come.

Then, just like that, they'd stopped.

She'd sat up in her bed in the darkness and decided that she was done crying about it. No matter what the other players did, they weren't going to run her off. They weren't going to make her quit. She told herself that now as she leaned her bike against her hip in front of the movie theater. Her mom told her she had to be better? Well, she was. Better than a bunch of boys who wanted to act like chowderheads, anyway.

"Alex! Alex Carlisle!"

She looked across the street toward the sound of her name and saw Sophie Lyons waving at her from the sidewalk outside Bostwick's.

"I hope you're here for ice cream," Sophie yelled.

"What else?" Alex replied.

"Good, you can sit with me then."

Alex gave her a thumbs-up, waited for the light to change, and walked her bike over to where Sophie was standing. There was still plenty of time before football. Alex knew from experience that a little Bostwick's soft serve usually made her feel better about everything.

"It would be a tragedy to eat ice cream alone," Sophie said.

"Should be against the law," Alex said.

Sophie Lyons was in Alex's grade at Orville Middle. Her sport was cheerleading, and it was just as competitive as football in their town. The cheerleaders often made it to state and sometimes national championships, both at the middle and high school level. Sophie was a gymnast first, with a private coach and everything. But she told Alex she enjoyed being part of a team even more. Cheerleading was the perfect combination of the two. Alex met Sophie last year, in sixth grade. The soccer team practiced on the field right next to the track where the cheerleaders held theirs. They started bumping into each other at the water cooler. Alex was a little shy, but Sophie's energy was infectious. Alex figured part of cheerleading was also having an outgoing personality.

They'd been friends ever since.

She was a little taller than Alex, white, with long, pin-straight red hair, lots of pink freckles on her cheeks and nose, and sparkling green eyes. She had a great smile, too. What Alex thought of as a happy smile. It took a lot to knock it off her face.

"Oh my god," she said. "I can't believe I ran into you. *Every*body is talking about you. You're a rock star!"

Alex grinned. They were in a back booth now. She'd locked her bike in the stand in front of Bostwick's. They were waiting for the line at the counter to get shorter so they could order.

"First of all," she said to Sophie, "I doubt that *every*body is talking about me. And second? I'm hardly a rock star."

"Okay, a football star then," Sophie corrected.

"I haven't even made the team yet," Alex said. "It'll be hard for anybody to think of me as a star if my name doesn't show up on the final list."

"Hold that thought," Sophie said, stepping out of the booth. "It's ice cream time."

Alex followed, and they ordered ice cream at the counter. Chocolate with rainbow sprinkles for Sophie, chocolate vanilla swirl with chocolate sprinkles for Alex.

Once they'd paid the cashier, they took their cups back to the table. Sophie looked like she had a lot more to say.

"We all think what you're doing is way cool, by the way," Sophie said.

"Who's we?"

"Everyone on the squad," Sophie said. "My mom. Other girls I've spoken to."

"For real?"

Sophie nodded as she swallowed a spoonful of ice cream.

"I haven't been online since I decided to try out," Alex said. "If people were talking, I didn't want to know."

"Most people have been nice," Sophie said. "Some have been idiots. But there will always be idiots."

Now Alex nodded, thinking back to two idiots in particular.

"Can I ask you something?" Sophie said.

Alex shrugged. "Sure."

"Are you scared?" Sophie asked.

"Between us?"

Sophie rolled her eyes as if to say: *Obviously*.

"Sometimes I think the thing that scares me most is making the team," Alex said.

She hadn't told anybody that. Not her dad, or Gabe, or Jabril. But Alex could tell Sophie really wanted to know. And she deserved an honest answer.

"Wait," Sophie said. "You put yourself out there to make the team and now you're scared you might actually *make* the team?"

"Crazy, right?"

Sophie thought for a minute. Then said, "No, I get it."

"I just keep thinking that if tryouts are this much of a grind, what's it going to be like when the season starts?" Alex said. "It's not like the other guys are suddenly going to welcome me with open arms or whatever."

"Is everybody against you?"

She told her Gabe and Jabril weren't.

"Twenty-four will make the team," Alex said. "If I'm one of the twenty-four, I'd have two on my side."

"And one more."

"Who?"

"Hello!" she said. "I'm gonna be on that field, too, remember? Rooting you on."

Alex hadn't thought about that until now. The cheerleaders would be on the sidelines of most games. She wouldn't be alone out there.

"Want me to give you a cheer?" she said to Alex.

THERE WAS A DIFFERENT VIBE TONIGHT. ALEX SENSED IT AND WAS pretty sure everybody else on the field at Orville High could, too. This was their last chance to impress Coach and Mr. Stiles and Mr. Wise, whom Coach had enlisted to help with player evaluations. There was a lot less chatter tonight while they went through passing drills. Even players who had been on last year's team clearly weren't taking anything for granted. There were no promises in football.

Alex thought she threw the ball well again, even better than Jeff Stiles had before her. But when she finished, something happened that bothered her. A lot.

Coach asked Lewis Healey to do some throwing, too. First time all week. Hadn't even been mentioned before this.

"I was watching you throw on the side the other night with Jeff. I liked what I saw from your arm," Coach said. "Let's see if you can throw to some moving targets as well as you can catch. Just for the heck of it."

Just for the heck of it.

"You up for that?" Coach said to Lewis.

Alex saw Lewis give her a quick glance before turning to Coach. "Everybody thinks they can play quarterback, right, Coach?"

He didn't throw for very long. But while he did, Alex had to admit, he showed off a good arm. *As good as mine*, Alex thought. *Not quite as accurate. But just as strong.*

She had enough to worry about already. She didn't need to add another thing to the list. Coach Mencken had just done it for her.

Maybe making him backup quarterback has been his plan all along.

Alex pursed her lips. She turned to the side, where she noticed Jabril standing a few paces away, arms crossed, feet planted in the turf. He smiled and nodded toward her as if to say, *It's okay. You got this.*

Before long, it was time for the scrimmage. Coach, Mr. Stiles, and Mr. Wise passed out nylon belts with flags attached. To Alex's relief, Lewis was at wide receiver. Jeff was at quarterback. Alex stood on the sideline with the boys who weren't starting on offense or defense. Though Coach had said they'd all get a chance to play.

Coach was in charge of the offense. Mr. Wise was setting the defense, which dominated the offense early in the scrimmage. Alex suspected that might happen. Coach hadn't put in any real plays yet. He said he'd do that next week, when real practices began. For tonight, it was as if they were playing in the schoolyard. Sometimes Alex could see Coach kneeling in the huddle and diagramming plays in the dirt.

Jeff Stiles and his running backs and receivers were struggling to make first downs. Every time they failed to execute,

Coach would make them go back to the twenty-yard line and start all over again. But no matter what they tried on offense, Jabril Wise was there to get in their way as middle linebacker, disrupting pass plays and run plays and looking perfectly willing to chase Jeff all the way to the parking lot.

He was the best player on the field by far. And he gave Alex one more thing to worry about, when and if Coach put her in at quarterback. Jabril may have been one of her only friends on this field, but unlike Lewis, he'd never throw a play as a personal favor.

Coach hadn't specified how long the scrimmage would last. But when the offense still hadn't scored after five or six possessions, Coach called out, "Miss—Alex . . . go in for Jeff."

He announced that this would be the last drive of the night. Jeff had gotten one chance after another to move the ball. Alex was getting just one. It wasn't fair. But then she remembered what her mom had said. *No one said it was fair.* Worrying about that wasn't going to help her get where she wanted to go, which tonight was the end zone.

Okay, she thought.

Okay.

Gabe and Lewis were her wide receivers. Perry Moses was at tight end. Tariq Connolly was the one running behind Alex in the backfield. Tyler Sullivan, the smallest player on the field and the only one faster than Jabril, was the slot receiver.

If I'm going to be a quarterback, I better be one now.

Coach had her hand off the ball twice to Tariq. He gained two yards both times.

Third-and-six.

In the huddle, Coach said what Alex had hoped he would.

"Gabe, get open over the middle."

Coach didn't have to explain that he needed to get past the thirty-yard line for a first down. They all knew that. And Alex knew she didn't want the last drive of the night—and the week—to come down to *fourth* down.

Jabril's dad didn't make things easy for her. He had Jabril come right up the middle on a blitz. None of the blockers did much of a job picking him up, so he was up in Alex's face in a blink.

But she had the presence of mind to pump fake—not much else she could do—and froze him long enough to scramble out of the pocket to her right. She hadn't had time to look for Gabe, because Jabril had been on her so quick. Alex picked him up now, though. He was running parallel to her as she ran toward the right sideline. She couldn't look, but she knew Jabril had had time to recover and was likely chasing from behind. But a yard before she would have run out of bounds, Gabe waved an arm at her, and she flung the ball sidearm to him. It wasn't perfect. It was a little low. Gabe went sliding to his knees and got his arms underneath the ball.

Clean catch.

First down.

She hit Tyler with a pass on the next play, and he ran fifteen yards with the ball before getting knocked out of bounds. Then she threw one to a wide-open Perry, and for a moment she thought he might go all the way until Jabril reached out and got his flag at the nine-yard line.

"First and goal," Coach said. "And for today, we're going to pretend there's thirty seconds left in the game and we need a touchdown to win. Just to dial things up."

Dial things up?

More than they already were?

Alex looked at Coach in the huddle.

"How many time-outs do we have?" she asked.

She thought Coach almost smiled. Just not quite.

"Smart girl," he said.

Or maybe he meant smart *for* a girl.

"One," he said.

She rushed a pass to Lewis on first down. He was open. She just missed him by being too anxious. The announcers on TV always talked about how the game slowed down in big moments for good quarterbacks. Only it had just gotten too fast for Alex. She told herself to slow down now, not get ahead of herself.

Just get the ball in the end zone.

If she did, she might make this team after all.

Maybe those weren't really the stakes. But it felt that way to her, and that was all that mattered.

She missed Tyler on second down. This one wasn't her fault. Tyler bobbled the ball slightly, and Jabril knocked it away for another incompletion.

The throw was to Perry again on third down. But Jabril blitzed. When Alex was out of the pocket this time, she decided to run for the score. Jake Caldwell was able to pick up Jabril and block him as Alex ran to her left this time. Alex turned the corner and thought she might make it, but at the last second she felt someone grab her flag. It was one of the safeties, Kerry Rhoades. Alex was still inbounds and immediately called time-out.

Fourth down from the one.

In the huddle, Coach said, "One shot at it. Run or throw?"

Alex didn't hesitate.

"Gabe," she said.

She looked at him and nodded. He did the same.

Coach said, "Push the boy guarding you a few yards into the end zone and then come back on a curl."

"Got it," Gabe said.

"No," Alex said. "*Get* it."

"You just get it to me," Gabe said, "and I'll take care of the rest."

Coach told Alex to back off the line into the shotgun formation. Cal Calabrese, the center, would snap her the ball. He'd done it a few other times on the drive. The snaps had been perfect.

This one wasn't. It came out of his hands low and hot, bouncing in front of Alex, immediately throwing off the timing of the play, especially Gabe's pass pattern.

But when she finally collected the ball and looked to her left, he was still open, Kerry Rhoades having played too far off him.

Still time to get it to him.

She never felt Jabril coming from her blind side, never computed that fumbling the snap had given him more time, too.

As she brought the ball forward, Alex felt Jabril's hand on her arm, then felt the ball come out of her hand and pop straight up in the air between them.

She reached for it. Too late. The ball fell right into Jabril's hands, as perfectly as if he were her intended receiver. Jabril took off in the other direction, flying for the end zone at the other end of the field. Alex took off after him, but it was like chasing the wind. Or a speeding car.

Alex kept chasing anyway, not giving up on the play. But Jabril kept putting more and more distance between them, never once looking back.

In that moment, Alex didn't imagine him just running down the field with the football under his arm. She imagined him running away with her chance of making the Orville Owls.

"I CAN'T BLAME THIS ON ANYBODY ELSE," ALEX SAID TO HER DAD. "I blew it myself."

They were in the car, on the way home. It somehow seemed like they'd been coming the other way just a few minutes ago, showing up at the high school for the first night of tryouts. It had happened as fast as Jabril recovering her fumble and running down the field.

"The only person who thinks one play is going to be the deciding factor is you," her dad said. "And by the way? It was a play at the end of the only successful drive the offense had all night. I know I'm not the most objective person in the world when it comes to you, but even if you include what happened at the end, you were the better quarterback tonight."

"I needed to be a lot better," Alex said, and slumped lower in her seat.

Coach had thanked them all for trying out before they left. He said that not everybody he'd watched over the past four nights had the same talent for football but that he would take into consideration how hard each and every one of them had competed.

"I could see how much you all wanted it," Coach Mencken said. "I know you all want to make this team. But not everybody can. Sometimes not everybody gets a trophy."

Then he thanked them all one more time and told them the roster would be posted on the school website at ten o'clock the next morning.

"Remember," he said. "Nobody lost this week. You all gained a lot of good experience out there."

In the car Alex said, "I just needed to complete that last pass."

They were making the turn into their driveway now. When the car had come to a stop, Alex started to get out.

"Wait," her dad said.

Her helmet was next to her in the back seat with her shoulder pads and the long-sleeve practice shirt she'd worn over them. Alex had changed into a black Steelers T-shirt and sweatpants but still wore her rubber cleats.

For a minute, she figured if she didn't make the team, she could wear the same shoes for soccer. The rest of the world called it football. It just wasn't the football she wanted to play. But then she remembered she'd missed soccer tryouts. She had nothing to fall back on. It was football or nothing.

Even if she could return to soccer, it would somehow feel like a consolation prize. Only because she'd had the most to lose by going out for football. If her name wasn't on that list in the morning, she was going to feel like a failure in front of the whole town.

"You need to explain to me again why you did this," her dad said.

He turned in the front seat to face her.

"You know why," she said. "I wanted to be a football player."

"And that's exactly what you were tonight," he said. "You

made plays, and you didn't give up, and you took your team down the field after Coach only gave you one shot to do that."

"Then I made the biggest mistake on offense that anybody made all night," Alex said. "On the last play anybody saw, starting with Coach. You know what he's going to remember? That turnover. The big T-O."

"No, he's not," Jack Carlisle said. "Unless he's forgotten anything he ever knew about football. What he *ought* to remember is that a great defensive player made a great play on the ball. That's not just football. It's sports."

Alex started to respond. Her dad held up a hand.

"I know your mom told you girls need to be better," he said. "I don't know about that. What I know is what I saw all week long. And Ed Mencken saw the same thing I did: that you're good enough to be on his team."

"I just wish I could have gotten us into the end zone," Alex said.

"And I wish I hadn't thrown the interception that cost us the championship game against Montville my senior year at Orville High," he said.

Alex knew the story of that game, because her father had talked about it all her life. Usually it would come after losing an important game of her own or coming up short in a big moment.

Alex opened her door again and started to get out of the car. Then she stopped herself and turned back to her dad.

"I never asked you," she said. "How long did it take you to get over that game?"

"You want the truth?" he said. "Because it doesn't line up with the pep talk I'm trying to give my daughter here."

"I always want the truth," she said.

"I'm still not over it."

Alex started up the stairs to take a shower and wipe off the night. Before she reached the landing, her dad asked if she wanted a hot fudge sundae when she came back down. Alex reminded him she'd already had ice cream today, but according to Jack Carlisle, you could never have too much ice cream. Alex thanked him for the offer but said she was going to turn her lights out early.

"Long night," she said to him.

"Long week," her dad said. "But you came through it like a champion."

"Not feeling it, Dad," she said. "You saw Coach had Lewis make some throws tonight. If all things are equal in Coach's head, I bet he makes Lewis the backup quarterback and adds an extra kid at another position."

"The one who should be the backup is Jeff the jerk," her dad said.

"You're being very immature," Alex said.

"I can't help myself," he said. "It's why your mom gave me that pillow in my office."

They both knew the one he meant. The pillow said, YOUNG ONCE. IMMATURE FOREVER.

"I wanted this so bad," Alex said, shaking her head.

"You *want* it," he said, smiling at her. "Present tense. You know what an old baseball guy used to say? It ain't over till it's over."

Then he walked over to where she stood at the foot of the stairs and gathered her in his arms, lifting her a few inches off the ground like he used to do when she was little. When she wasn't a football girl. Just his little girl.

"I wish you were the coach," Alex said into his shoulder.

"I feel like one up there in the stands," he said. "You just can't hear the things I'm shouting inside my head."

After she'd washed up for the night, she thought about calling Gabe. Or Sophie. Or even her mom. But then she decided she didn't need any more pep talks.

She shut the door to her room, turned off the lights, and closed her eyes. But as soon as she did, all she could see was the ball floating up between her and Jabril, and Jabril taking off with it down the field.

Welcome to football, she thought.

The next morning, Alex awoke next to her stuffed Simba. It made sense. He was the one who ultimately gave her the courage to talk to her dad about football tryouts. Now, after four days of exhausting drills and practice, only one decision stood in the way of Alex's dreams. It came down to this. Either Alex would make the team and work toward becoming a better player, or she wouldn't, and everything would come to a cold stop.

It was nine a.m. The list went up at ten. The wait was agonizing, but Alex passed the time by having a bowl of Cheerios and watching ESPN.

One episode of *First Take* later and it was five minutes to ten.

Alex took the stairs two at a time up to her bedroom and grabbed her laptop off the desk. She opened it up on her bed, right next to Simba, her good luck charm. So many athletes had them, and now she finally understood why. But would it be enough?

Alex typed in the school's website at one minute after ten. A few clicks in, she found the seventh-grade football team roster. The names were listed in alphabetical order.

Alex let her eyes wander near the top of the list. To the *C*s.

The fifth name on the list was Rick Carbury.

The sixth was Alexandra Carlisle.

After that, the names blurred.

She made it. She was on the team.

Now she could finally say out loud what she'd been thinking.

"I'm a football player."

11

THE FIRST DAY OF SCHOOL THE NEXT WEEK WAS ALSO THE FIRST DAY
of football practice.

By now Alex knew the first day of school was always the same,
a combination of nerves and excitement. She was curious to see
what her classmates had been up to all summer. Some came back
a few inches taller, or with a new haircut or wardrobe. Since Alex
had grown up in Orville, she already knew most of her classmates. But there was still the sense, every year, that a new adventure was beginning for all of them.

This year was different.

All she could think about was that football was starting for
her at six o'clock on the field behind Orville Middle.

"Is this when they start tackling you?" Sophie said on their
way to the cafeteria. Alex was grateful they shared a lunch period.

"No clue," Alex said. "We're going to have two practices
a week. Even my dad doesn't know how much contact we're
allowed to have. They've cut down on contact during the week
for NFL teams, too."

"Good to know," Sophie said.

Now Alex laughed.

"So you're saying you could get tackled tonight."

"I could get tackled tonight."

"By boys in football gear who're probably way bigger than you."

"I'll be wearing the same gear."

"I know, but there's a difference," Sophie said.

"'Cause I'm a girl?"

"I mean, yeah," Sophie said. "Our bodies are different. Certain places need more protection, if you know what I mean."

Alex just laughed again.

"Seriously, though," Sophie continued, "do you think the guys are going to go easy on you? Y'know, to avoid tackling you?"

Alex hadn't considered that. She'd figured, if anything, they'd want to tackle her harder. Wear her down so she'd quit the team. But the alternative was that they'd be worried about hurting her and getting in trouble for it. It was a whole new concern she didn't know how to deal with.

When they finished eating, Sophie said she'd forgotten something in her locker and would see Alex in history, their first afternoon class. There were still ten minutes left of lunch, so Alex stayed at the table and pulled out *To Kill a Mockingbird*, their first reading assignment for Ms. Isaacs's English class. Ms. Isaacs had sent out an email last week to her seventh-grade classes with the syllabus for the term. She'd said if anyone wanted to get a head start on the reading, they could. So Alex had grabbed her dad's worn paperback from their shelf at home and read the first fifty pages. Already, she loved the character Scout.

Alex thought Scout had some lion in her, too.

She was concentrating so hard on her reading that she didn't notice Jeff Stiles and Lewis Healey until they'd sat down across from her.

"Hey, guys," she said.

She'd barely spoken to either one of them during tryouts. After the first night, there was really nothing to say. It was possible they'd been posting about her on social media, but Coach made it clear that he didn't want to read about his team on "Facegram." He said that whatever his players had to say to each other, they should say it to their faces.

Now Alex was face-to-face with Jeff and Lewis. Jeff got right to it, leaning closer in so the kids at the other end of the table couldn't hear. He was smiling. Alex thought the smile was phonier than his dad's.

"You know that he had to take you, right?" Jeff said.

"Who had to take me?" Alex said. She wasn't going to make things easier for him, even though she knew exactly who he was talking about.

"No way Coach was going to cut the only girl who tried out for the team," Jeff said.

"I earned my spot," Alex said. *More than you earned yours.*

She closed her book.

"Yeah," Lewis said. "Go with that."

"It was just easier for Coach to keep you than cut you," Jeff said.

"And why's that?" Alex said in a calm voice.

If anybody in the cafeteria was watching they would have thought the three of them were having a friendly chat over lunch. But it was like everything else. Alex wasn't backing down.

Sometimes she felt like a new person, the Alex who stood up for herself and went after what she wanted.

"Coach just didn't want to be accused . . ." Jeff stopped himself, as if not quite knowing how to finish the sentence.

"Accused of not giving a girl a fair chance in sports?" Alex said. "Something along those lines?"

Jeff scoffed. "You have your own sports."

"And, what, you guys have football?" she said. "Is that a law somebody passed?"

"Do you really think the other guys want you on the team?" Jeff said. "Forget Coach. You think we want the hassle of having a girl around?"

"Did you take a vote?" Alex said.

"If we did, you'd lose in a landslide," Jeff said. "All you can do is screw up our team."

She looked past them to the big clock on the wall. It was time for her to get to history. And get out of here. Away from them.

"How am I going to do that?" she said.

"By being *on* the team," Jeff said.

"So, what do you think I should do?" she said theatrically.

Jeff and Lewis said the same word at the same time.

"Quit."

"What's wrong?" Alex said. "Scared of a little competition, Jeff?"

She picked up her book and stood.

Jeff's face was angry now. "As far as I'm concerned," he said, "I *have* no competition."

Alex just shrugged in response.

"Why are you really doing this?" Lewis asked.

"Why are you?" she shot back.

"Because I want to play football," Lewis said.

"Yeah, well," Alex said, "so do I."

Jeff shook his head. Alex couldn't tell whether he was disgusted or just frustrated with how monumentally dumb he thought Alex was being.

Alex knew she should walk away now. They clearly weren't going to change their minds about her. They certainly weren't going to change hers.

But sometimes you couldn't help yourself.

"If I intimidate you so much, maybe *you* should quit," she said.

Now she turned and walked away. From behind her she heard Jeff say, "Starting quarterbacks don't quit, *Alexandra*."

He and Lewis started to laugh then. Alex kept walking, as if she couldn't hear them, or didn't care. Coach hadn't told them who'd be starting, but Alex guessed it would be Jeff. His dig was targeted directly at her, but she didn't let it get to her.

In *The Lion King*, Simba's dad, Mufasa, said that being brave didn't mean you went looking for trouble.

But she already had.

THERE WAS NO TACKLING THE FIRST NIGHT OF PRACTICE.

But there was the second night.

Alex was the one who hit the ground hardest.

The guys on defense had spent most of the first few nights of Owls practice working on the fundamentals of tackling.

"Tackling in my day used to be just tackling," Coach Mencken said. "But in the modern world of football—the one we're living in now—we know a lot more about how to protect our heads."

Mr. Wise worked on proper technique at one end of the field with the defensive players. At the other end, Coach and Mr. Brewster, whose son Corey was their best offensive tackle, worked with the offense. Mr. Brewster, who'd played tackle himself for Ohio State, worked with the linemen. Coach worked with the receivers and the backs. He ran through the basics, too, starting with things as simple as handoffs.

Once Alex was positioned behind Cal, their center, she quickly discovered that the footwork required for a QB was more complicated than it looked from the stands or on TV. It involved pivoting and timing and making sure you were as accurate placing the ball in a receiver's hands as you were throwing a pass.

Jeff Stiles had been practicing these moves since the time he'd started playing organized football. It was different for Alex. She was getting on-the-job training for the first time.

Once, when she turned a beat too late and muffed a handoff to Tariq, she heard Jeff say, "Being quarterback isn't as easy as it looks, huh?"

Alex didn't give him the satisfaction of turning around. She just got back behind Cal, ready to take the next snap. Coach told her to keep going until she got it right. But she could feel heat beginning to spread on the back of her neck and across her cheeks. Mostly because, in this case, she knew Jeff was right.

Being a quarterback was more than just throwing the ball down the field, or running with it when you got the chance.

Every time she made a less-than-perfect handoff, Alex found herself wondering what it was going to be like in a game situation, when everything sped up and a ball on the ground could mean a recovered fumble for the other team. It might even decide the outcome of a game.

At the end of the second night of practice, they played a seven-on-seven drill.

Jeff had taken most of the snaps, mixing running plays with passing plays. There were three guys in the line, two wide receivers, and Tariq in the backfield. The defense had two linebackers and two defensive backs.

The running plays and passing plays were pretty basic, as were the blocking patterns. Coach said he was just trying to "put the offense up on its feet a little."

The ball was at midfield for the offense when Coach announced they were going to have one last drive and that Alex was going in as quarterback.

"Seven-on-seven," Coach Mencken said. "But let's see if we can get six to end the night."

Meaning a touchdown.

Even now the objective was the same: get the ball over the goal line.

Coach was calling the plays. He let Alex throw on first down, and she completed what she thought was a pretty sweet pass to Gabe. The second play was a run to Tariq. He was supposed to take the handoff and run past Alex and behind Cal up the middle. But Tariq was overeager. If it had been a real game, he probably would have been called for illegal motion and coming out of his stance before the ball was snapped.

But there was no whistle now. He practically ran right up Alex's back as she was turning to hand him the ball. He was still in a crouch, and the ball bounced off his left shoulder pad into the air.

Then it was on the ground.

Fumble.

Busted play.

Alex reacted quickly, though, scooping up the ball as the play officially became what Coach called a "fire drill." During a fire drill, you were supposed to give up on the play and improvise. You were supposed to make something out of nothing.

Alex ran to her right, feeling the pursuit behind her. She didn't have to look to know Jabril would be right on her heels. And even having only played with Gabe in scrimmage-type situations a handful of times, she knew he'd be reacting to the play, too. Sure enough, he came running in her direction.

She gave a quick look over her shoulder and saw Tariq trying to block Jabril. But it was too little too late. Jabril got past him and started coming toward her fast.

Of course.

He was always on the ball, wherever it was.

Make a play.

"Alex!"

It was Gabe. She'd almost forgotten he was there.

The offense was wearing red pinnies tonight. She saw a flash of red, saw that Gabe was running right along with her toward the sideline. If she didn't release the ball now, she'd be forced to run out of bounds, and the next play would be third-and-long.

She sidearmed the ball in Gabe's direction just as Bryan Chen, one of their cornerbacks, came plowing into her.

He must have left Lewis when he saw Alex take off and, like Alex, was trying to make a play, either by batting the ball down or bringing her down.

She was so focused on Gabe that she didn't see Bryan until it was too late. Bryan would tell her later that he tried to veer off and miss her completely. But he was at full speed, and it was impossible to miss her or pull up.

The next thing she knew she was flying, feeling as if she were spinning in the air like helicopter blades.

She finally landed on her stomach. Not her head or her shoulder or throwing elbow.

That was a good thing.

The bad part was that as soon as she touched the ground, she felt all the air come out of her at once. She couldn't breathe. Coach was always talking about how you had to focus on the fundamentals.

Alex rolled over and sat up, trying to catch her breath.

When she finally got some air in her lungs, she peered up and saw Gabe and Jabril standing over her. Coach was there, too. So was Bryan Chen, helmet off and tucked under his arm, looking worse than Alex felt.

And Alex felt as if she'd fallen out of her bedroom window.

"Didn't have a good angle when you stuck the landing," Coach said. "Did you hit your head?"

Alex wasn't surprised at the question. She followed football passionately. She knew how concerned, even obsessed, everybody was with head injuries, whether you were playing seventh-grade football in Orville or for the Pittsburgh Steelers.

"My head's fine, Coach," Alex said. "Just got the wind knocked out of me is all."

"I am *so* sorry," Bryan said.

"It was a clean hit," Alex said. "What my dad likes to call a real good lick."

She actually didn't know what kind of hit it was. Just that it was the hardest she'd ever been hit in her life. She'd collided with soccer players before. But nothing like this. She'd tumbled to the ground plenty of times on the soccer field.

Not. Like. This.

Welcome to football.

Sophie had asked about getting tackled. Well, now Alex had been. Her dad often quoted the boxer Mike Tyson, who once famously said, "Everybody has a plan, until they get punched in the face."

It occurred to her now that she didn't know whether she'd

completed the pass or not. She looked up at Gabe, who offered her his hand to help her up.

That's when she spotted the football in his left hand.

"You caught it?" she said, more than a little surprised.

She could see his smile behind his facemask. "I mean, it *was* a little behind me," he said, pulling her up.

Alex laughed and found that nothing hurt when she did.

"I was kind of occupied," she said, "as you might have noticed."

Coach told her to take the rest of the practice off. Alex tried to tell him she was fine, but he told her they were going to end the scrimmage on that play anyway.

"You made something out of nothing," Coach said. "Heck of a play."

Alex thanked him and went to get her water bottle out of her backpack on the sideline. She didn't look at Jeff Stiles or Lewis Healey or any of the other guys who didn't want her on the team. She'd made a play. Coach had acknowledged it in front of everybody. That was enough for her.

She knew she was probably going to be sore tomorrow, even if she wasn't right now.

But she'd found out something about herself tonight, on a six-yard completion in a seven-on-seven practice game, no less.

Found out something and maybe proved something to herself, too.

Girl could take a hit.

13

"OKAY, WHAT HURTS?" ALEX'S DAD SAID.

They were home now, and Alex had taken what felt like the longest hot shower in history. Now she was lying across the living room couch in sweats.

"Other than my pride?" she said.

"Over what? Getting knocked down?" Jack Carlisle said. "Everybody gets knocked down."

They were eating enormous ice cream sundaes, courtesy of Alex's dad. Jack Carlisle was a firm believer that ice cream could cure just about anything.

"My whole body," she said. "But I could have finished the scrimmage if Coach let me."

"My girl," her dad said. "Tough as nails."

"Nah," she said. "Just couldn't let them get me down."

"I can't believe you completed that pass after the Chen boy flattened you."

"Best completion I never saw," she said with a chuckle.

"Well, you've been wondering what it was going to be like when someone popped you a good one," he said. "Now you know."

"Yeah," Alex said. "And if I ever get to play in games, I'll probably get popped like that more than once."

Her dad put down his bowl and said, "When. *When* you play in games. Keep that chin up."

Alex stuck out her chin, as if to prove she was following his orders.

After they finished their ice cream, Alex gingerly got up from the couch. She had to get some homework done. It was the first week of school, but that didn't mean teachers went easy on them. Before she headed upstairs, her dad said, "You sure you're okay?"

"It was a little scary," she said, "being in the air that way. You don't know what kind of a crash landing you're gonna get."

"You gave me quite a scare," he said.

"It was just football, Dad," she said. "I wanted to be a football player. Nobody made me do this. Nobody seems very happy that I *am*. But I knew what I was getting myself into. It was my call."

"But if you ever change your mind," her dad said, "and decide that it's not worth it, that's your call, too."

"I know," she said.

"It doesn't matter what anybody else thinks," he said. "Just what you think."

"I know that, too."

She went up to her room, shut the door, leaned against it, closed her eyes, and smiled. She hadn't lied to her dad. She *was* okay.

But she was sore.

All-over sore.

From her first hit.

But not her last. If she did get real playing time this season, the players bearing down on her weren't going to try to miss, like

Bryan. They weren't going to pull up. The guys on the opposing defense might feel the same as her own team about a girl being on the field. Maybe they would *want* to flatten her the way Bryan Chen did tonight.

Then she thought back to what Sophie said. About how the boys might try to avoid tackling her because she's a girl. As much as it hurt taking the hit earlier, it was also a relief. These guys might not want her on the field, but getting hit tonight was evidence they'd do anything necessary to win, tackle whoever they had to.

Which meant Alex might be taking a few more hits this season.

Was it worth it?

Yeah, she told herself after her first official night of tackle football. Yeah, it was.

14

THE NEXT PRACTICE WASN'T UNTIL SATURDAY, A WEEK BEFORE THE
season started.

Coach said there would be only two practices per week. But
because their first game, against Latrobe Middle, was scheduled
the following week, Coach got permission to have an extra practice, as long as it didn't involve contact.

Fine with me, Alex thought. Now that she'd been hit once, she
wasn't intimated by a little rough play.

But at school on Friday, she found out there were all kinds of
ways to get hit.

Hard.

Sophie packed her own lunch on Friday. The cheerleaders could
only meet during lunchtime that day; otherwise they would have
been sitting in the cafeteria with Alex.

"You're not the only one getting ready for the start of the season," Sophie told her earlier in the day.

"I've got this feeling," Alex said, "that next Saturday you're
going to have a lot more action on the field than I am."

"We'll still be cheerin' for ya!" Sophie's teammate Kim said
to her, smiling.

When Alex did get to the cafeteria for lunch, she saw that

Gabe and Jabril were sitting with Cal Calabrese and Perry Moses and some of the other players on the team. It was Alex's team, too. It should have been the most normal thing in the world for a person to join their teammates at lunch. But there was, Alex knew, nothing normal about her place on this particular team. Nothing normal about what she was doing, and not just on the football field. From what Sophie and the other girls had told her, she knew she was the talk of Orville Middle. There were some who might find that exciting. Alex wasn't one of them.

There was an empty seat at the table where some of the girls' soccer team was sitting. The girls who would have been Alex's teammates this year had she gone out for soccer instead of football. Lindsey Stiles, Jeff's cousin, was there. Ally McGee. Carly Jones. The best goalkeeper in their league, Mallory Bidwill, was there. And there was lots of chatter and laughter going on at the table. Their area sounded like the bus used for road trips last season.

Alex filled up her plate with mac and cheese, some salad, and a bread roll and walked over to where they were sitting with her tray.

As soon as she got close, the chatter stopped. All the girls turned to stare in her direction.

At first, Alex thought they might be looking at something behind her, but that was wishful thinking.

It was Mallory who piped up and said, "You must have the wrong team."

Then Lindsey. "In case you didn't notice, *your* team is over there."

She pointed to where Gabe and Jabril and the guys were having lunch.

"Are you serious?" Alex said to them.

"Do we look like we're joking?" Lindsey said, a sharpness in her tone.

Suddenly, the entire cafeteria went quiet. Alex saw Jabril's head snap up from his table, looking in Alex's direction. It was as if she'd sent up a smoke signal, and Jabril was reading it from a mile away. She could see him reaching for his backpack, ready to back her up, but she waved him off, not wanting to draw any extra attention to herself.

Alex had never anticipated her old teammates would box her out like this. They acted as though trying out for football was a personal affront to them. Like she'd intentionally snubbed them for the fun of it. Why couldn't anyone understand this was about doing something for herself? It made her angry now. But worse, it made her feel something else.

Alone.

Finally, she walked away, feeling all eyes in the cafeteria bore into her.

She swept through the swinging doors, found an empty classroom, and ate lunch by herself.

15

Alex still didn't feel like part of the team. She was no doubt *on* the team. It just wasn't how she knew a team should be. With everyone having your back, celebrating your triumphs and picking you up after you got knocked down. She had Gabe and Jabril on her side. But it wasn't like they could go around campaigning in Alex's favor. A lot of the boys had proven to be as hardheaded as Alex. Unwilling to accept her as part of the team. Keeping their distance. Only interacting with her when Coach called a play that made it necessary. Although she was out on the field for every practice, there was a part of her that still felt as if she were watching football from the sidelines.

But she wasn't going to quit.

She'd come too far just by making the team. She wasn't about to let a weasel like Jeff Stiles win by walking away now.

Alex had always thought she was pretty realistic about herself. Her strengths and weaknesses, stuff like that. She knew she wasn't great at a lot of things. And until now, she'd had no idea if she could be great at football. But she was determined to try.

No going away. No giving in. No giving up.

She and her dad had just finished dinner. He headed upstairs to do some work in the converted bedroom office upstairs. Alex was in her room reading, waiting for the start of *Thursday Night Football*, when the doorbell rang. Alex yelled up to her dad that she'd get it.

When she got downstairs and opened the door, Gabe was standing there.

Alex grinned.

"Are you lost?" she said.

Behind him she saw his bike leaning against one of the pillars on their porch.

"Jabril and I just had ice cream in town," Gabe said.

"Thanks for inviting me," she said, joking.

He smiled back and shrugged. "My bad."

"I get it," she said. "You're just afraid to be seen with the girl QB."

"Come on," Gabe said, rolling his eyes playfully, "you don't really think that."

He was wearing a navy Penn State T-shirt with gray shorts and flip-flops. When Alex tried to wear flip-flops riding her bike, they usually fell off.

"Nah, I'm only teasing," Alex said.

From the top of the stairs they heard Alex's dad say, "Are you going to invite Gabe in, or treat him like he's here to sell raffle tickets?"

"Oops," Alex said. "*My* bad."

"At least you've got manners, Mr. C," Gabe called up to him.

"I try so hard with her," came Jack Carlisle's voice from above.

Alex just rolled her eyes as she shut the door behind Gabe.

She led him through the kitchen and out to the back patio.

It was early evening, and the sun was setting behind the trees in their backyard. Alex loved this time of day, when the sky turned gray.

Trying to regroup on her manners, she asked Gabe if he wanted anything to drink. He said he was fine and apologized for just stopping by without calling or texting first.

"I don't know," he said. "Once I left Bostwick's it was like my bike came here on its own."

"Like one of those cars that drives itself," Alex said.

They sat and watched the fireflies floating around in the backyard.

"I guess I kind of just wanted us to talk like we used to," he said.

"We still talk," Alex said.

"But there's always other people around," Gabe said. He blew out some air. "Not that I'm that great at talking anyway."

"I'm not much better."

"Girls are better at talking," Gabe said.

"I wouldn't say that," Alex said. "Never came naturally to me."

She turned to look at him. "Is there something specific you wanted to talk about?"

She noticed him frowning, looking a little uncomfortable.

"I guess I'm still trying to figure out why you did all this," he said.

All this, Alex thought.

There it was.

"Not much to understand," Alex said. "You've always known how much I love football."

"But a lot of girls love football and don't try out for the boys' team," he said.

He was talking to her but staring out at the yard. *Too embarrassed to make eye contact*, Alex thought.

"It's only a boys' team because no girl ever tried out," she said.

"Until you," Gabe said. Alex sensed his agitation. But she wasn't sure what exactly was causing it.

She turned her chair to face him now, the leg making a scraping sound on the concrete.

"What are you really asking me, G-Hills?" she said.

It was the nickname she'd given him. One she only used when it was just the two of them, talking the way Gabe said they used to.

Now he turned his chair. No scraping noise. A lot of things came easy to Gabe.

Just maybe not this conversation.

"I guess I want to know if you still think it was worth it," he said to Alex.

"We haven't even played a game yet!" Alex said, laughing.

"Come on," he said. "You're one of the smartest people I know. You know what it's going to be like . . ."

"So, what," Alex said, "I'm a smart person doing a dumb thing?"

"I didn't say that."

"Kind of what I'm hearing," Alex said. "Makes me wonder whose side you're on." She turned her face away from him, crossing one leg over the other.

"Come on," he said. "You know me, Alex. You know I'm your friend first. It's just . . ."

"Just what?" she said, twisting to look at him again.

"I shouldn't have to be on anybody's side," he said. "I've only ever been on my team's side."

"Same with me," Alex said, not sure what he was implying or why she always felt the need to defend herself.

They sat there in silence for a while, except for the crickets and cicadas and katydids and whatever else was out here. She could remember asking her dad what was making all the noise when she was young. He'd smiled and told her it was her own special orchestra.

"It's just hard sometimes," Gabe said.

Alex couldn't help it. She laughed. "Hard for *you*?"

"I'm not saying it's the same for Jabril and me as it is for you," he said.

"You guys are taking heat, right?"

Gabe shifted in his seat. "A little, yeah."

"You sure you can handle it?" Alex said. But if she was being honest with herself, she didn't care about his answer. It couldn't come close to what she'd been facing the last few weeks.

Alex could see Gabe making fists in his lap.

"It's like, we don't talk about football anymore," he said. "We've got our first game coming up, and all anybody wants to talk about is having a girl on the team."

"You're saying I'm a distraction," Alex said.

Gabe didn't even hesitate. "Yeah."

Alex started to say something, but Gabe went first. "But, I mean, is it even worth it if you don't get to play?"

"You think I'm not good enough to play?" she said.

She wondered if Gabe was speaking on behalf of the rest of the Orville Owls.

"No," Gabe said. "It's not that. I think you're better than Jeff. But it won't make a difference to Coach."

"You don't think he's going to play me . . ."

"No."

Just like that.

"Even though you think I'm better."

"Yeah."

Alex smiled now. It just came over her, like how the porch lights came on automatically.

"Why are you smiling at that?" Gabe said.

"Because my mom told me this happens a lot," Alex said. "Even when a woman is better at something than a man."

Gabe stood up.

"I should go," he said. "My mom doesn't like me riding my bike in the dark, even though I've got one of those reflector lights."

"I'm glad you came by," Alex said.

Gabe managed a grin. "You sure?" he said.

She stood up now and told him she'd walk him to the door.

"I'm still your friend," he said.

"But you liked it better when you were just that and not my teammate," she said, a little sad.

Gabe gave a sheepish grin. "I can be both."

"You sure?" Alex said, giving his shoulder a little jab.

He gave her a long look and said, "Just remember, for everything you do see, there's a lot you don't."

She watched him get on his bike and ride to the end of her

driveway before taking a left toward home. She watched him until the light attached to his handlebar disappeared around the corner.

She stood there and kept hearing the last thing Gabe had said to her.

There's a lot she didn't see.

She wasn't sure if that made her feel better or worse.

GETTING READY FOR THE FIRST FOOTBALL GAME OF HER LIFE WAS A
process.

"I wouldn't spend this much time getting ready for a school
dance," Alex said to her dad.

"You hate getting dressed up for dances," he said.

"This is different," Alex said.

They were in her room. She had neatly laid out her uniform
on her rocking chair before going to bed the night before. Helmet,
pads, jersey, football pants, and spikes. The game was scheduled
for eleven, at Orville Middle. Coach Mencken had asked them all
to be there an hour early. He said if anyone was even a minute
late, they'd be taking laps around the field.

Alex was all ready to go by nine a.m. sharp.

"I'll tell you something else," she said. "It was a lot easier getting ready for soccer."

"Waaa, waaa, waaa," her father said. "What happened to no
crying in football?"

He was leaning against her doorframe, holding the coffee
mug Alex had given him for Father's Day. On one side it read,
WORLD'S BEST DAD, and on the other it said, ALMOST POSITIVE. It
was the only mug he used.

"You miss it?" he said. "Soccer?"

"I thought I missed being with the other girls," she said. "But they don't seem to miss me."

"They're just hurt you left the team," he said. "Like you dumped them."

"It's not like that, Dad," she said. "I'm just trying something new. Only now my old teammates like me about as much as my new ones."

"The season's just starting," he assured her.

Alex looked at herself in the mirror in full gear. "I just wish I were more excited."

"Come on, kiddo," he said. "As soon as you step out on that field, you're gonna realize it was all worth it."

"I'm not so sure," she said. "It just makes me mad, you know? How the guys act like I'm trying to steal their lunch money or something."

He came over and sat down on the edge of her bed.

"I've told you about Billie Jean King, right?" Jack Carlisle said. "How she wasn't just a tennis player but a trailblazer for women in sports?"

"Totally," Alex said. "The more I read about her, the more I want to be like her."

"Well," he said, "she's said a lot of great things. But to me the best thing she ever said was that pressure is a privilege."

"I remember that one," Alex said.

"And don't you forget it," he said. "That's the way we've got to approach this thing."

Alex smiled. *"We?"*

"Yeah, we," he said. "I'll be playing the game right along with you."

"Like I'm going to play," she said, skeptical.

As it turned out, she would.

17

SHE ENDED UP WITH NO. 3. HER DAD SAID IT WAS THE PERFECT number for her.

"You're a triple threat," he said. "You can pass, you can run." He grinned. "And you obviously threaten the heck out of those boys."

Even though they were in Steeler country, they were close enough to Penn State that the Owls wore similar colors: blue jerseys with white numbers. But when Alex got out on the field at a quarter to ten, she wondered if she'd have the opportunity to get her uniform dirty today. Or ever.

Most of the boys were already out there. Jabril was the only one who jogged over, football in hand, asking if she wanted to warm up with some soft-tossing. He didn't mention anything about what happened in the lunchroom the other day. Almost like he knew Alex wanted to put the whole episode behind her. Once again, Alex was grateful to have someone like Jabril in her corner.

Gabe was down near one of the end zones, tossing in a triangle with Tariq and Perry. Jabril noticed Alex staring at them.

"He's fine," Jabril answered her unspoken question.

They both knew he meant Gabe.

"I didn't know he wasn't until he came to my house the other night," Alex said.

"After ice cream? Yeah. He told me."

"What was all that about?" Alex asked.

"He doesn't like to talk about it," Jabril said, "on account of the boy doesn't like to talk about anything very much. But I think some of the other guys are messing with his head."

"Because of me," Alex said. It wasn't a question.

Jabril nodded.

"How come they're not messing with *your* head?"

Jabril's smile spread across his face as he looked straight at Alex.

"By now you ought to know that nobody messes with any part of me."

Alex smiled back. It was no wonder Coach had named Jabril team captain. Not only was he one of the best players on the team, he also had the most confidence and treated everyone with respect. He was the definition of a team player.

They saw the team from Latrobe Middle arriving then. Their jerseys and helmets were red, which made sense, given that their team was the Cardinals. That was about all Alex knew about them. She hadn't heard anything about the other teams in their league either. Plenty of the guys on the Owls had played Latrobe Middle last season. Not her.

"Are they any good?" Alex asked Jabril.

They'd finished throwing the ball back and forth.

"Real good last year," he said. "The quarterback is a stud."

Jabril thought for a minute. "Alex," he said finally. "Alex Mattis. But a boy Alex."

"What are the odds?" Alex said.

"Not as great as you being the Alex on our team," Jabril said. "And math is my best subject."

Five minutes before kickoff, Coach gathered his players around him in a team huddle.

"No speeches today," he said. "No speech I ever heard affected what I did or how I did it. Play hard. Play clean. And just know that the next play you make—or don't—is the one that could change everything."

The Owls won the toss. Coach chose to kick off, which is what most coaches did in the pros. It was usually preferable getting the ball at the start of the second half.

On the third play of the game, Jabril led an all-out blitz on Alex Mattis. He came from behind the Cardinals' quarterback just as he was bringing his arm up to pass. But Alex Mattis wasn't able to get forward motion on the ball before it was out of his hand and on the ground. Jabril fell on it, recovering the fumble, and just like that the Owls had a first down at the Cardinals' twenty-five-yard line.

When Jabril jogged back to the sideline, Alex threw him a big, swinging, enthusiastic high five.

"That quarterback isn't the stud in this game," Alex said. "You are."

"All we got was the first break," he said. "Now let's see what we can do with it."

Jeff Stiles handed the ball twice to Tariq. He got two yards each time. Third-and-six. Jeff dropped back to pass, with Tyler wide open in the left flat. But he overthrew him. Badly.

Fourth down.

"Too close to their end zone to punt," Jabril said.

Keeping her voice low, so only Jabril could hear, Alex said, "We should run the exact same play again. Jeff can't possibly airmail him twice in a row."

"You sound like one of those announcers commentating on the game," Jabril said.

"That's what my dad always says."

They ran another pass play. To Alex's disappointment, not the same one they'd just run. It was a crossing pattern to Gabe over the middle. Jeff had enough time to throw, and it was clear Gabe was going to be open as he made his break. But Jeff rushed the play, throwing too soon and too far behind Gabe. The ball was nearly intercepted. But it didn't matter. The Owls hadn't done anything with the first break of the game, and they turned the ball right back over to the Cardinals.

Neither team made big mistakes over the rest of the first half. But there weren't many big plays, either, especially on offense. Then, in the last minute before halftime, Alex Mattis got some time to throw. One of his wide receivers got behind Bryan Chen, and Alex threw a perfect, deep ball. The wide receiver briefly bobbled it but managed to hold on, then took off down the field, while Bryan and Jabril tried to chase him down.

6–0, Cardinals.

That's how you throw a football, Alex thought to herself, having watched the throw with admiration. *That's how you throw one at any age.*

In seventh-grade football you could go for the extra point by running or throwing for the conversion. Two points were given if you kicked it, just because not many seventh graders could kick a ball through the uprights from twenty yards away. Alex thought she could do it if she practiced. Playing soccer for so many years would give her the edge. Sometimes she thought that if she proved to Coach Mencken she could do it, he might let her on the field. She used to watch YouTube videos of US Women's Soccer star Carli Lloyd kicking field goals from fifty yards away. But Alex was afraid if she asked Coach for a chance to be a placekicker, he might stop seeing her as a quarterback.

And that was the way she saw herself.

Even on the sideline.

She looked down the row of her teammates. The second strings and offensive line. Gabe was among them, watching the field, and Alex wondered if he purposely decided to stand all the way at the other end, away from Alex. She couldn't figure out if he was giving her the cold shoulder or just randomly wound up on that side of the field.

On the field in front of her, Alex Mattis rolled out to his right, faked a throw, then dove over the goal line for the conversion point to make it 7–0, Cardinals.

Coach didn't scold Jeff for how poorly he'd played in the first half, even though he *had* played badly, completing just one pass, to Perry Moses. It meant he had as many completions to their team as he did to the Cardinals, because he'd thrown a bad interception at the start of the second quarter.

"We've been given a gift here," Coach said during halftime. "And the gift is that we're only down one score without playing anywhere near our best. So let's get out there and unwrap that gift as soon as we get the ball."

Of course, their first drive of the second half turned out to be a disaster. First, Lewis Healey twisted his ankle throwing a block on a sweep and had to come limping out of the game. Then, on third down, Jeff scrambled out of the pocket toward Gabe, who'd broken his pattern and come back to Jeff's side of the field.

But at the last second Jeff pulled the ball down and decided to run.

As he did, the ball slipped out of his hand and bounced behind him. Jeff couldn't find it right away, but the Cardinals' middle linebacker did, picking up the ball cleanly and running thirty yards, untouched, for the end zone, making it 13–0, Cardinals.

One minute into the second half.

The Cardinals took the Owls' gift for their own.

Jeff blamed Gabe when they both got to the sideline.

"I pulled the ball down because you took off just as I was about to throw," Jeff said.

"I was coming back to block," Gabe said. "We already had linemen past the line of scrimmage trying to block for you. If you'd thrown, they would have called illegal receivers downfield."

Jeff stubbornly shook his head.

"You're wrong," he said to Gabe.

"You couldn't see them," Gabe persisted. "I could."

Jeff turned to Lewis Healey, sitting on the bench, his leg stretched out in front of him.

"You saw, right, Lewis?" Jeff said.

Lewis looked at Jeff, then Gabe. He probably knew Gabe was right. But he didn't want to give up Jeff.

"Tough to see anything from the bench," he said to Jeff.

"Whatever," Jeff said, wiping sweat off his brow. "I was just trying to make a play."

"Enough chatter," Coach said, walking over to them. "Make a play when we get the ball back."

Jeff completed a couple of passes on the next series. But after one first down, the Owls had to punt. After that, it was all Alex Mattis, as the Cardinals went on an eighty-yard drive. He finally threw a touchdown pass to his tight end, who ran for another conversion.

20–0, Cardinals.

With two minutes left in the game, it looked as if the Cardinals were about to score again. But Jabril made a great defensive play, chasing down Alex Mattis in the open field and slapping the ball out of his hands to recover it for the Owls. Jabril didn't care what the scoreboard said. He'd told Alex that he was willing to keep playing all the way to midnight.

Jeff started to run back on the field with the rest of the offense, but Coach put a hand on his arm to stop him. From where she stood on the sideline, Alex could see Coach telling him something but couldn't make out what it was. Jeff shook his head, and Coach patted him on the back and walked over to where Alex was standing.

"Go in for Jeff," he said.

Alex stood there, not sure if she'd heard him correctly.

"You want me to go in . . . to the game?" she said.

"Miss Carlisle," Coach said, "I'd get out there before I change my mind."

In one swift movement, Alex shoved her helmet on and ran toward the huddle.

She was in the game. The first one of the season, no less.

Even if it was just for a couple of minutes in a blowout game, she was now the quarterback of the Orville Owls.

Just one thought came to mind.

Pressure.

Privilege.

18

THE OWLS HAD TWO REALLY GOOD TIGHT ENDS. ONE WAS PERRY Moses, their starter. But Danny Farrell was even bigger than Perry, almost as fast, and even played linebacker sometimes. They both could really catch.

Coach was alternating them now, having one or the other bring in the play he wanted them to run from the sideline. Alex knew she should have asked Coach what the first play was. But she was so excited she'd forgotten.

Perry had her covered.

The first play was a quick pitch to Tariq, with Alex in shotgun formation.

Alex stood a few yards behind Cal Calabrese, waiting to take the snap, heart thrumming in her chest.

She told herself to collect the snap, turn, and pitch it to Tariq. Like connecting dots. Let Tariq and his blockers do the rest.

Cal snapped her the ball. She didn't rush the pitch. Just calmly tossed the ball to Tariq. She was still soaking in the moment of being on the field. Playing her first game. She'd never quite understood what an out-of-body experience was, but this had to be it. The way it felt as though she were floating above herself, watching from the sky.

Tariq ran to his right, and Alex raced in front of him to become a blocker herself, even managing to slow down the Cardinals' left defensive end.

Tariq ran for eleven yards.

First down.

Danny Farrell came in with the next play: Pass to Gabe over the middle. Just a quick slant. Take the snap. Don't hesitate. Throw it. She did. It wasn't her best throw, and it went a bit behind Gabe. But he reached back with his right hand, tapped it, and made the catch. He took a hard hit from the Cardinals' middle linebacker but was able to hold on. Ten more yards. Another first down.

Suddenly they were at midfield with only a minute left on the scoreboard.

Most important, the Owls were driving for the first time all day.

Coach still had all his time-outs. He probably didn't expect to use them, since the score was 20–0, Cardinals. But he called one now and waved Alex over to the sideline.

"We're not gonna win this game," Coach said to Alex. "But if we can put the ball in the end zone, we'll have won something out here today."

"Okay," Alex said.

"We won't have time to run Perry and Danny in and out with the plays," he said. "So here's your next three. Screen to Tariq, another quick slant to Gabe, then an out pattern to Gabe. Got it?"

"Got it, Coach," Alex said.

Alex swung her head to the side and caught Sophie's eye from where she stood with the cheerleaders in their own formation.

Sophie gave Alex a thumbs-up, and Alex nodded before jogging back onto the field.

The Cardinals blitzed on the next play. They weren't letting up just because they had the lead. If anything, they wanted to pre-serve their shutout. But the blitz had played right into the Owls' hands. It was a perfect play . . . if you could get the ball away.

Alex waited until the last second, a tidal wave of red about to crash her to the ground. And she did end up on the ground. Got creamed. But first she released the ball to Tariq.

It was a clean hit, from the defensive end Alex had blocked on first down. He was trying to knock down the pass. He missed it but still managed to knock Alex flat.

Alex knew the expression about running into walls. This time it seemed the wall had run into her.

The next thing she heard was the whistle ending the play. Next thing she *saw* was Cal Calabrese reaching down to help her up.

"You okay?" Cal said.

"Yeah," Alex said, jumping up.

"You hurt your head?" Cal asked.

Alex tipped back her helmet and knocked on the side of her skull.

"Only thing that doesn't hurt."

Cal told her Tariq had caught the ball and run for twenty yards before getting knocked out of bounds. But Alex was barely paying attention. She was too caught off guard that a teammate who wasn't Gabe or Jabril was helping her up. Was talking to her. Was treating her like anyone else on the team.

She and Cal jogged up the field to join their teammates in the huddle. Alex *did* hurt, especially on her left side. But not enough to come out of a game she'd worked so hard to get *into*. She looked up at the scoreboard.

Forty-two seconds left.

For a moment, she couldn't remember the next play she was supposed to call. Then it came to her. Slant to Gabe. This time she put the ball where she was supposed to, and Gabe caught it in stride. In fact, he did more than that. The real commentators always talked about guys running in space.

Gabe Hildreth was running in space now, away from the cornerback covering him, around their safety, turning the corner, on his way to the end zone.

The Owls were on the board.

So am I, Alex thought.

Gabe didn't celebrate once he crossed the goal line. They were still losing, 20–6, and their record would still be 0-1. Alex didn't celebrate either.

She pushed aside whatever awkwardness was between her and Gabe and ran down to where he stood in the end zone, giving him a quick high five.

"Now it's worth it," she said.

19

ALEX DIDN'T SMILE IN THE HANDSHAKE LINE. AS HAPPY AS SHE WAS about that last drive and putting some points on the board, they'd still lost the game.

She hated when athletes on some of the pro teams did one of those stupid touchdown dances when they were down by a lot.

She wasn't that kind of player.

Coach gathered them around him one last time and reminded them it was just one game in a long season, and there was still plenty of football to be played. He told them not to hang their heads, and to learn from the mistakes they'd made. Build on the positives. And that he'd see them at practice on Tuesday.

The only player to congratulate Alex before everybody headed to the locker room was Jabril. Gabe waited until the others were far ahead before joining their conversation. Alex tried not letting it get to her head. Sophie had to stay with her team for now but promised Alex they'd meet up later.

"You were playing some ball there at the end," Jabril said, clapping her on the shoulder.

"Yeah," Gabe said. "The positives Coach was talking about? Mostly they were you, AC."

"I didn't throw that touchdown pass to myself," Alex said, shoving Gabe with her hip.

They were standing behind their bench, drinking cups of Gatorade. The other players had rushed to get inside. Not Alex, Gabe, and Jabril. They were basking in the moment, even if the Owls had been out of the game since early in the second half.

"You guys were having some fun there at the end," Jabril said.

"Winning would be fun," Alex said, kicking up dirt with her cleat.

"Next week," Jabril said. "Coach is right. Long season."

Gabe left first, helmet under his arm, toward the boys' locker room door. Even though they'd played well together at the end, Alex still felt things were strange between them. She wondered if the only reason he'd stayed behind was because he didn't want to blow off Jabril. Or possibly Jabril had made him come over. It was as hard saying no to Jabril as it was blocking him.

"You want to hang later?" Jabril said.

"You, me, and Gabe?" Alex asked.

"I can't speak for him," Jabril said, offering a sheepish smile. "You just gotta give him some space and time to figure out how he wants to roll with all this. He just wants everybody to be on the same side of things."

"And I don't?" Alex said.

"Like I said," Jabril said, "give him time. Some people need more than others to come around."

"Right," Alex said. "Long season."

"So, you want to do something later?"

"I promised Sophie I'd hang with her," Alex said.

"She can't be more fun than me," Jabril said.

Alex laughed.

"And just remember something," Jabril said. "When you're away from all of us, and it's just you and Sophie? You're allowed to feel good about what you did out there."

He bumped her some fist.

"You know, Jabril," she said, "you're an even better friend than you are a football player."

"And don't you forget it."

"I'll try," Alex said.

"You know what they say about football," he said. "No medals just for trying."

Alex and Sophie decided to go for ice cream at Bostwick's, mostly because they couldn't think of one good reason why they shouldn't. Jabril was right. Alex was allowed to celebrate a little bit, even if they'd lost.

"First we get ice cream," Sophie said as they walked off the field together. "Then we go back to your house and binge Netflix."

"I'm down," Alex said.

"Mind if I sleep over?" Sophie asked. "My brother's having some of his dopey friends over."

"Sure," Alex said, thinking it'd be nice to spend time with a friend who wasn't on the team.

While Sophie and Alex washed up in the girls' locker room, Alex's dad waited for them in the parking lot. The girls sat in the back seat of the car on the way to Bostwick's, and Jack and

Sophie talked animatedly about the way the game ended. Alex reminded them that all she did was quarterback one touchdown drive, not win the Steelers another Super Bowl.

"Yeah, you're right," Jack Carlisle said. "I'm sure there were thousands of other twelve-year-old girls across America doing what you did today."

"I'll probably be back on the bench next Saturday," she said.

"Maybe you will, maybe you won't," her dad said. "But you sure gave your coach something to think about."

"Dad," Alex said, "you're the one who's always telling me how much football coaches hate quarterback controversies."

She could see him grinning in the rearview mirror.

"Well," he said, "there's always an exception that proves the rule."

Alex and Sophie grabbed a corner booth. They both ordered the same thing: chocolate swirl with rainbow sprinkles. Sophie still had her hair up in a tight ponytail with blue and white ribbons.

"Sorry you wasted your time," Alex said. "There wasn't much to cheer about until the end."

"Are you kidding?" Sophie said. "That was so dope, what you did out there."

Alex couldn't help but agree. It *was* cool. And she shouldn't minimize the accomplishment.

"It was, wasn't it," Alex said. "From now on, you can call me the football queen."

"Yaaas, queen," Sophie said, pretending to bow down.

They both laughed. It felt good to be away from football for a little while. Away from all the drama.

"I'm glad I was there to see it," Sophie said. "Dude, you are seriously good."

"I had to be," she said. "If I'd messed up, I'd never live it down."

They sat, eating their ice cream. Alex felt safe with Sophie. Knew Sophie had her back, even though that didn't help Alex very much in football. But Sophie didn't judge. If Alex wanted this, she wanted it for her. Simple as that.

"What do you think will happen next week?" Sophie asked.

"Jeff plays, I sit," Alex replied.

"Well, that stinks."

"Not if he plays well," Alex said. "Because that means the team's doing well."

"But what if it could do better with you out there?" Sophie said.

"Not my call," Alex said. "But honestly? Part of me thinks Coach only put me in today to get it out of the way. So no one will wonder if he'll ever give the girl a chance."

Alex was sitting against the back wall, facing the door. Sophie must have seen her face change.

"What?" Sophie said, eyes wide.

Alex jerked her chin. "Check it out," she said.

Sophie looked over her shoulder. Jeff Stiles and Lewis Healey had just walked in.

Gabe was with them.

"Well, this isn't good," Sophie said, turning back to Alex.

Alex frowned. "You can say that again."

The boys ordered and got their ice cream and took the front booth. Alex could see Lewis limping slightly on his ankle. She didn't think they'd seen her yet, so she edged her way a little closer to the wall to shield herself from view.

"This is so crazy," Sophie said, reacting to Alex. "You guys are on the same team."

"Jeff thinks it's his team," Alex said, her voice lower now. "And I'm sure he's chafed that I did well today."

"You did and he didn't," Sophie said. "Big-time."

Alex blew out some air.

"Let's just finish our ice cream and leave," she said.

"Netflix awaits us," Sophie said. "A friend you can count on."

"Gabe's still my friend," Alex said, a little defensive. Though she wasn't quite sure why.

"Doesn't look that way right now."

Alex got up first. When they passed by the table where Jeff, Lewis, and Gabe were sitting, Alex gave them a quick wave.

"Hey, guys," she managed to say.

Jeff was on one side, Lewis and Gabe were on the other. Jeff smirked, keeping his eyes on them instead of looking at Alex.

"Look who it is," he said sarcastically. "The star QB."

"Not so much," Alex said. "Just got lucky and made a few plays. Mostly thanks to Gabe."

She shot him a quick glance, hoping to catch his attention. But he looked as if he wished to be anywhere on the planet except sitting in this booth.

Alex felt Sophie tug on her arm. Like, *Let's get out of here.*

"Don't be modest," Lewis said, sounding as sarcastic as Jeff. "They'll probably be selling No. 3 jerseys at Dick's this week."

"What, not yours, *Josiah*?" Sophie said.

It was Lewis's actual first name. Nobody at school ever used it, because they knew he hated it. Lewis was his middle name.

"Aw, are you here to give Alex a cheer?" Lewis mocked.

Alex ignored him.

"Hey, Gabe," she said, figuring maybe a more direct approach would help. Might shame him into realizing he was making a huge mistake.

"Hey," he said in a small voice, staring into his bowl of ice cream.

"Let's go," Sophie said. "This is about as much fun as watching grass grow."

But Jeff wasn't finished. He looked up at Alex and said, "Anybody can look good at garbage time."

They all knew what garbage time meant in sports, even though Alex had always hated the expression when announcers used it on TV. Garbage time usually meant backups got a few minutes to play at the end of blowout games like today's.

"The defense was barely trying," Jeff said.

Clearly, he wasn't letting go so easily.

Alex shifted her eyes to Gabe, wishing he would say something. Anything. But he was still hunched over his bowl of ice cream, averting his eyes from Alex and Jeff.

"Let's go," Sophie said again.

But Alex stood her ground.

"You know, Jeff, I finally figured out your problem," she said.

"That you shouldn't be on our team?"

"No," she said. "You can't take it that I'm better than you."

"Seriously?" he said, his voice rising. "You think one touchdown pass means you're better?"

Alex smiled now.

"I wasn't talking about football," she said.

20

AFTER SOPHIE'S MOM PICKED THEM UP AND DROPPED THEM BACK AT Alex's house, Alex decided not to tell her dad what happened at Bostwick's. He was still floating on air from watching Alex play today, like he had been the one to throw a touchdown pass to Gabe.

Her buddy Gabe.

Or so she'd thought.

Alex and Sophie were barely through the front door when Jack Carlisle started up about the first Steelers home game tomorrow. In the same breath, he asked if Alex had brought back ice cream for him. She held up the to-go bag in her hand.

"Of course," he said, "I don't need ice cream to make my day better than it already is."

"Dad," Alex said. "We lost!"

"Minor technicality," he said.

When Alex and Sophie were upstairs, Sophie said, "He really is over the moon."

"That's why I'm not going to spoil it by telling him about a maroon like Jeff Stiles," Alex said.

"Maroon?"

"It's one of my dad's expressions," Alex said. "Like moron, but better."

"By the way?" Sophie said. "Don't let that *maroon* spoil this moment for you, either."

"He tried pretty hard," Alex said, smirking. "But he was about as good at that as he was at football today."

They were on Alex's bed watching *To All the Boys I've Loved Before* on her laptop when her mom called from California. Alex guessed she was calling to see how the big game went.

Alex motioned for Sophie to keep watching and headed downstairs and out to the back porch. She passed through the living room, where her dad was watching the Penn State–Ohio State game.

"Soooooo. How did it go?" her mom said.

Alex told her.

"Wait," her mom said. "You got to play in the first game *and* threw a touchdown pass? Get out of town!"

"I know, right? It was almost like I knew what I was doing out there," Alex said.

"Sounds like you proved something today."

"Not to my teammates," Alex said, before telling her mom what happened at Bostwick's.

"Nothing you could ever do would impress that boy," her mom said. "And you're not doing this to impress him anyway."

"I know."

"He's just mad because you showed him up," her mom said. "Even if you apparently didn't shut him up."

"I didn't tell Dad," she said. "He just would've gotten mad."

"Sounds like you got a little mad yourself."

"The one I should be mad at is Gabe," Alex said. "I can't figure out how to handle things with him."

"Well, let's talk about that," Liza Borelli said. Alex's mom wasn't a psychologist, but sometimes she sounded like one.

Football was never going to be her mom's strong suit, even if she was getting better at talking about it. But she was much more skilled at discussing growing-up things.

"He's always been such a good friend to you, honey," she said to Alex. "It just sounds to me as if he's under some tremendous peer pressure and isn't handling it particularly well."

"But he told me he'd be my friend no matter what."

"Maybe he won't be until the season is over."

Alex bristled. "Friendship isn't supposed to be a seasonal thing, like football."

"You're right," her mom said. "It shouldn't be. But keep in mind, people process things in different ways."

"Jabril says he just needs time and space."

"Jabril sounds like he knows what he's talking about."

Alex sighed.

"Honey," her mom said, "you had to know it was going to be like this. It always is when somebody's the first to try something. People are threatened by it."

"But why?"

"Because people generally like things to stay status quo," her mom said. "In this case, in Orville boys' football."

"Even when you're good at something?"

"Especially when you're good," her mom said.

Alex heard the sliding door behind her. Her dad poked his head out. Alex pointed to the phone and mouthed, *Mom.* He nodded and went back inside. Her parents still talked sometimes, if not all that often. And not today. Maybe her dad wanted to give Alex the chance to tell her mom about the game herself.

"People keep asking me if it's all worth it," Alex said. "I keep telling them it is. But sometimes I'm not so sure."

"Honey, there's always a cost when you chase a dream," Liza said.

"Is there more of a cost when you're a girl?"

Her mom's sigh was so loud Alex imagined she didn't even need a phone to hear it all the way from California.

"At present? Yes," she said. "When I was growing up, people used to say it was a 'man's world.' Smart people, especially smart women, knew that wasn't true. But it didn't change the fact that we had to fight a little harder to get what we wanted."

Alex took in some air, let it out.

"Going after what I wanted cost me your father," she admitted.

The thought hit Alex like a two-hundred-pound linebacker.

"Wow," Alex breathed, her voice soft now. "Was it worth it to you?"

She didn't know where the question came from, but there it was.

"Chasing *my* dream cost me my marriage, absolutely," Alex's mom said. "But I'd like to think it hasn't cost me you. Or we wouldn't be having this conversation, right?"

"Right."

"Listen," her mom said. "I have to get back to the hospital. There's a patient I need to look in on."

Not the first time this had happened. Alex knew it wouldn't be the last.

"Let me leave you with something," her mom said. "You know how little I know about football."

"Uh huh," said Alex.

"But I think I know you well enough to know that you wouldn't have taken this on if you didn't think you had a chance to be great. Not just good. Great. So go do that, okay?"

"Okay."

"And don't let a toolbox like Jeff what's-his-name think he can take you down."

"Toolbox, Mom?"

"Hey, you gotta give me credit for trying. But I have to run. Love you and I'm proud of you!"

Alex said "I love you" back and hung up the phone.

21

FOOTBALL SUNDAYS AT HEINZ FIELD ALWAYS FELT SPECIAL FOR Alex, ever since the first time her dad started taking her six years ago. Alex never grew tired of watching the Steelers play live.

While Alex loved so many things about her dad, and their life in Orville, there had always been something magical about their trips to Pittsburgh.

Despite Alex's jokes, her dad didn't need a son with whom to share the Steelers. He just needed her. He wanted to be with her, cheering at the good plays, groaning at the bad. Running for a soda and hot dog or soft pretzel at halftime.

Steelers against the Browns today.

Today football was pure fun.

Oh, she wanted her team to win. That was always the goal. She knew she'd be upset if they lost, and the ride home would feel a lot longer than the ride there. But she wasn't experiencing the kind of nerves she'd felt yesterday against the Cardinals. Today was more of a celebration. Right from the time they entered the Heinz Field parking lot to tailgate with old friends. Her dad brought his portable grill, as always. His job was to fire up the burgers and dogs and bratwurst and chicken wings for what Alex called their "Steeler Family." They'd been tailgating together for as long as Alex could remember.

Mr. and Mrs. Chaplin brought amazing salads for every home game. Mr. and Mrs. Paoli made the desserts. The Paolis were from Latrobe, and their son Tommy was the same age as Alex. By now, they felt like football cousins. But then, the whole thing felt like a family reunion. When the Steelers played on Monday night, Jack Carlisle always brought his daughter with him—even though Alex had school the next day and they sometimes wouldn't get home until well after midnight.

"Wouldn't be the same without you," her dad explained to her. "We're a team."

They were a team, starting another home season watching *their* team. The weather was perfect. So was the game, pretty much. The Steelers were ahead, 24–7, by halftime and never let up after that. A lot of people started to leave late in the fourth quarter, with the Steelers up 38–14 by then. Not Alex and her dad. They always stayed until the very end. Avoiding the rush ended up working in their favor, as traffic getting out of Pittsburgh wasn't as bad as it could have been.

Alex never minded sitting in traffic with her dad, though. If anything, she preferred it, because it kept the day going. And this had been a particularly good day, not just because the Steelers had won in a breeze. She had watched the game from a different perspective today. Paid closer attention to what the quarterbacks were doing. She'd watched their footwork closely, watched the way they viewed the field when they dropped back to pass. How they'd look one way for the longest time before turning in the other direction to find an open receiver.

Having taken some hits of her own now, Alex studied the way

they'd go into their slides when they ran out of the pocket and into the open field. In other words, she studied how to avoid getting sacked.

On one play, the Steelers quarterback went into his slide even though he could have gained a few more yards by running. Afterward, Alex's dad leaned in toward her ear and said, "Sometimes you have to know when to tackle yourself. Even if you're not afraid of taking a hit."

"I'm not afraid," Alex said.

He patted her knee and said, "My girl."

They'd left the stadium and were crossing over the city line into Orville when Jack Carlisle said, "This ought to be an interesting week of practice for you."

"They're all interesting," Alex said.

"You earned some respect yesterday," he said, "whether they want to admit that or not."

"Nothing I ever do will be enough for the guys who don't want me on the team," she said. "And they all pretty much don't want me on the team."

"And that's not fun, I know," he said. "But you were still having fun out there yesterday. I could tell."

She decided to tell him then about what had happened at Bostwick's. What Jeff had said about garbage time and her sly comeback.

Jack Carlisle shook his head and snorted. "What *he* said is what's garbage," he said. "Everybody on the field was still trying. Still trying to show their coaches they deserved to be out there. It was still eleven against eleven out there."

"You know what I saw today?" Alex said. "I saw the players on both teams supporting their teammates, especially after one of them made a good play."

They were pulling into their driveway now.

"It'll get better," her dad said.

"You don't know that."

"Okay," he said. "Let me put it another way: it can't get any worse, right?"

Wrong.

22

THE NEXT GAME FOR THE OWLS WAS THAT SATURDAY, AGAINST THE Palmer Lions.

And it turned out the players on the Lions didn't like having a girl on the field any more than the Owls did.

Maybe less.

It started during warm-ups.

Alex did some extra stretching on the fifty-yard line after the team had gone through their regular calisthenics. Her dad was the one who'd recommended it. Nothing major. Just basic stuff. But he'd drummed into her head that any athlete—"even an old dude like me"—was dumber than rocks not to stretch before engaging in physical activity.

Two of the Lions players came jogging past her.

No. 14 and No. 58.

None of Alex's teammates were close by to notice. Shocker.

"Hey," No. 14 said to Alex. "We heard about you."

Alex didn't respond. She was lying on her back, extending one leg and then the other into the air to stretch her quads.

"Hope we don't make you cry today," No. 58 said.

They were keeping their voices down, presumably not wanting to get in trouble with their own coach.

"Or run to your mommy," No. 14 said.

For some reason, they both found that hilarious. But she thought it was pretty dumb—and uninspired, honestly.

She rolled over into a sitting position.

"My mom lives in California," she said. "So that would be difficult."

She thought that would stop them, but it didn't. She gave a quick check of the field, hoping to see Jabril somewhere nearby. Not to be her protector. Just to interrupt their little chat so she could concentrate on what really mattered: winning this game.

"We were wondering," No. 14 said. "When you're not playing, do they give you pom-poms and have you lead some cheers?"

They busted up laughing at that.

Then No. 58 took a step closer to Alex, leaned down, and said, "Hope to see you on our field later."

Alex stood up to her full height, a few inches taller than No. 58.

"Not just yours," she said.

"What?"

"It's not just your field," she said. "It's everybody's. Even mine today."

Then she turned and walked toward the Owls' bench. She was filling up her water bottle at the cooler when Jabril said, "What was all that about?"

"Just a little pregame chirp," Alex said. "Nothing I couldn't handle."

He smiled one of his wide Jabril smiles.

"Still waiting to see something you *can't* handle," he said, slapping her five.

• • •

It turned out that No. 14 was the Lions' quarterback, and No. 58 was an outside linebacker. And, to Alex's great amusement, neither was living up to their smack talk. Jabril intercepted the second pass No. 14 threw and returned it thirty yards for a touchdown. No. 58 and his teammates on defense were helpless against stopping the Owls' running game. The guys in the offensive line kept opening up huge holes for Tariq, as he ripped off one big gain after another. Alex knew Jeff must have wanted to throw the ball more, but there was no point. Not the way the Owls were controlling the game on the ground. So Coach continued calling handoffs to Tariq and the other running backs. By halftime, it was 20–0, Owls.

The second half wasn't much different. No. 14 continued having a very, *very* bad day. Or maybe, Alex, thought, this was a normal day for him. On the Lions' first drive of the second half, No. 14 fumbled at his own ten-yard line, and Bryan Chen picked up the ball and ran in for an easy touchdown. Tariq ran the ball in for the conversion. Now it was 27–0. Alex wanted to feel bad for the quarterback. But she couldn't. Not after the way he'd acted before the game. He was just another bully. In or out of football uniforms. She'd already had her fill of it in football, and they weren't even finished with the second game of the season.

It was 33–0 for the Owls, two minutes into the fourth quarter, when Coach told Alex to go in for Jeff. It was a different kind of blowout game this week, with the Owls leading. Maybe this was the way it was going to be all season. She would only get a chance to play if they were winning by a mile or losing by a mile.

Alex didn't care.

She just wanted to play. Whether the game was on the line or not.

"It's gonna be pretty straightforward stuff," Coach said. "You'll do what Jeff spent most of the game doing, which means handing off the ball. I'm not one of those coaches who thinks he can impress people by running up the score. We haven't done that today. Our last two scores have come off our defense. Mostly we just want to run the clock and get the heck out of here. Got it?"

"Got it," Alex said.

On second down, she tried a quick pitch to Tariq. But he started running before properly securing the ball and flat-out dropped it.

Alex was close enough to the play to get to the ball first. And she was smart enough not to attempt to pick it up and run in traffic. Not with two Lions defenders right on top of the play. So she fell on the ball, right before their linemen fell on top of her. She felt players trying to rip the ball away from her before the ref started untangling the bodies in the pile.

Then she felt something else. Somebody shoving her face-mask into the ground, twisting it a little, as if forcing her to eat dirt and grass. It was dark inside her helmet, and hard to breathe.

"How's our field *taste*?" she heard somebody say from above her. No. 58.

Once the whistle blew and the refs dismantled the pileup, she was able to shift her body and pull the front of her mask out of the turf. She clutched the ball to her chest in victory.

As she got to her feet and handed the ball to the ref, she saw No. 58 staring at her. She stared right back.

"You got something to say?" he said to Alex.

"Yeah, I got something to say," she said. "Scoreboard."

Coach called time-out, and Alex could see him waving her over to the sideline.

"Been in a lot of those pig piles myself," he said. "Something happen at the bottom of that one?"

"Nothing I can't handle," she said, repeating Jabril's mantra.

"You want to serve up some payback?" Coach said.

Alex looked up at Coach through her helmet. "What did you have in mind?" she asked.

Coach told her the play he wanted her to run.

"You like?" he said.

"Love," she said.

She was in the shotgun. After she took Cal's snap, she rolled to her right. No. 58's side of the field. It was supposed to appear as if Alex was planning to throw the ball, probably to Gabe. No. 58 wanted to sack her before she did. He flew toward Alex. She stopped, made a perfect pump fake with the ball, watched as No. 58 kept flying right past her.

And took off.

For a minute, she thought she might have enough open field to go all the way. She had the speed, for sure. But then she saw one of the Lions' safeties coming across the field, cutting off her angle. Alex didn't tackle herself in this case. Just ran out of bounds to avoid a hit.

The safety didn't stop. He plowed into her at full speed, sending her crashing over the edge of the Lions' bench. She could hear the ref blowing his whistle before she even hit the ground, yelling about unnecessary roughness. When she rolled up into a sitting position, she saw the ref signaling that the safety was out of the game. Done for the day.

As soon as Alex stood up and felt the pain in her knee, she knew she was done for the day, too.

No point in bluffing.

She was hurt, all right.

After she limped her first few steps, Jabril came sprinting across the field to help, but she waved him off. She didn't want to be assisted off the field. Nevertheless, she knew she had to come off. And out of the game.

She saw Coach Mencken and the Lions' coach talking to the ref at midfield. When the Lions' coach spotted Alex, he came over and apologized, saying he didn't coach his guys to make dirty plays like that.

"Thanks, Coach," Alex said. "But I can take it."

When she got to the bench, Jabril knelt down next to her and said, "Which knee?"

"Left," Alex said. "I'll live."

"Nearly scared *me* to death," Jabril said.

Dr. Calabrese, Cal's dad, had Alex pull up her pant leg. They both observed a colorful bruise beginning to form, and some swelling. But after having her put some weight on her leg and do a few range-of-motion movements, he said he didn't think it was anything serious and suggested she ice it for the rest of the game.

"Hey," Dr. Calabrese said. "No more injuries." He was smiling.

"I hear you," Alex said.

Holding the ice pack to her knee, Alex turned around to where she hoped her dad still was in the stands. He'd remained in his seat, even though she knew he was probably anxious to come down and check on her himself. When they were in the car on the way home, he told her what he'd really wanted to do was come down and have a chat with the safety.

"That would've been a conversation worth live-streaming," she said.

"It was a cheap shot," he said, anger visible in his expression.

"The cheapest," Alex said. "And it probably won't be the last."

"When are these boys going to get over themselves?" Jack Carlisle said.

"If it had been a close game," Alex said, "I would have asked Coach to put me back in there before it was over."

She saw him turn his head slightly, so she could see him in the rearview mirror. His face had softened.

"My girl," he said.

"You think you'll ever get tired of saying that?" Alex said.

"Not anytime soon," he said. "How's the knee?"

"That's like the fifth time you've asked me."

"What can I say, I'm an involved parent," he said.

They had just turned the corner onto their street.

"You think you'll be okay to practice on Tuesday?" he asked.

"What do you think?"

"My girl," he said again.

After she showered and changed into gym shorts and her favorite US Women's Soccer T-shirt, she came downstairs to ice her leg again and watch college football with her dad. The swelling, she saw, hadn't gotten any better. But it also hadn't gotten any worse.

About an hour later, Jabril called to see how she was doing.

He was the only teammate who did.

24

M<small>OST DAYS</small> A<small>LEX</small> <small>ATE LUNCH WITH</small> S<small>OPHIE IN THE CAFETERIA.</small> S<small>OME</small> days she ate with Jabril. Some days with both.

Gabe had started eating with other teammates, not just Jeff and Lewis. They sat at the same table, on the opposite end of the cafeteria from where Alex usually sat. She didn't want to be near them. They didn't want to be near her.

On Monday it was just Alex and Jabril. Sophie had stayed home from school with a bad cold.

Jabril asked Alex if she had talked to Gabe over the weekend, but Alex shook her head no. They really had nothing to talk about. On the field, they got along fine. But that was all the relationship they had right now.

Alex asked Jabril if he'd discussed any of this with Gabe, and Jabril said he had.

"What did he say?" Alex said.

"That he didn't want to talk about it," Jabril said.

Alex felt herself deflate. "Then neither do I," she said.

"You two are friends."

"Not right now," Alex said. "But I'm cool with that. I really don't have any friends right now besides you and Sophie."

"That can't be true," Jabril said.

"I wish I were lying," Alex said. "Playing football turned out to be a *way* bigger deal than I imagined."

"A lot of this is because of Jeff," Jabril said.

Alex waited for him to elaborate.

"Not many people, other than Lewis, liked him that much before we all joined the team last year."

"So why is everyone so enamored with him all of a sudden?"

"Can't explain it," Jabril said. "But he got Lindsey all fired up, and then she got the girls' soccer team fired up."

Lindsey. Jeff's cousin. She and Alex had never been all that close, even as teammates. They were two of the better players on the girls' team. But Lindsey was as self-absorbed as her cousin. Alex determined it must be a family trait.

"Somehow Jeff and Lindsey have convinced people that you think you're better than the other girls in school," Jabril said.

"Well, that just means they're spreading lies," Alex said. "I swear, J, if I'd known it was going to be like this, I would have stuck with soccer."

"Nah, that wouldn't've been you," he said. "You had to try. And now it turns out you got more than try in you. You got game."

"I don't want you to take any heat because of me," Alex said.

Jabril's lips curved up into a smile. The look he gave Alex made her feel as though somehow everything was going to be all right.

"Like a real good friend of mine says," Jabril said, "I can take it."

Sophie was well enough to come to school the next day. Jabril was eating in the library, working on a history assignment he hadn't finished the night before. He didn't say why, but Alex knew. He'd been watching *Monday Night Football*.

Alex and Sophie filled their trays with food and walked over to the long table of seventh-grade girls in the middle of the lunch-room. Some Alex recognized from the soccer team, and others were on Sophie's cheerleading squad.

"You ready?" Sophie said.

Alex nodded.

She and Alex sat down at two empty seats at the end of the table.

Everybody else at the table except the two cheerleaders, Isabella Martinez and Ava Bianchi, stood up and walked away. For a moment Alex thought maybe Isabella and Ava might leave, too. But to her relief, they stayed and even smiled at Alex.

"Whatever happened to sisterhood?" Sophie said.

"Seems to me it just got up and left," Alex said.

Alex's dad came home early so he could run through some con-ditioning exercises with Alex in the backyard before the Owls' practice that evening. They were meeting at Orville High tonight, after the varsity players had their practice. Jack Carlisle had Alex throw a few balls and run some routes to prove that her knee was back to full strength.

"Look like a QB to me," he said. "Know why? 'Cause that's what you are now. You can throw, you can run. And even the ones who won't admit it know that. Keep that in mind. You're a threat because you're good."

Alex warmed up in a T-shirt and her football pants. It was almost time to go upstairs and get into her Owls uniform. Usually there was a feeling of excitement when gearing up. Just not today. She felt as if she'd already taken her first hit of the day, from the girls' soccer team.

She told her dad what had happened at lunch.

"I didn't do this so everybody would be talking about me," she said.

"You don't have to tell me," he said. "You've never been one to draw attention to yourself."

"I know!" she said. Then more seriously, "I didn't want to admit it, but it's starting to get to me."

He cupped a hand on her shoulder and smiled down at her.

"You'd tell me if it got to be too much . . ." he said, the concerned father coming out in his tone. "There shouldn't be more things making you unhappy about this whole experience than happy."

"There aren't," she said. "Being good at football makes me feel good about myself."

"I don't say this often enough," he said. "But you're one of the strongest people I know."

"Dad," she said, embarrassment flushing her cheeks.

"I'm serious," he said.

And as much as they liked to joke around, Alex knew he was being sincere this time.

She nodded, acknowledging the compliment, then said, "Okay, enough of the mushy stuff. Go long."

Alex's dad ran out, and she threw him a great deep ball. When he caught it, he spiked the ball and went into one of his goofy touchdown dances.

She was ready for practice now.

THE THING WAS, IT WASN'T AS IF GABE *WASN'T* TALKING TO ALEX.

But they both knew they weren't really talking *to* each other—not at practice, not at school. Not the way they used to. A lot had happened since Alex announced she was going out for the team. An awful lot.

But she never expected this from Gabe.

She felt bad for him. She did. She could see how much pressure he was under from the other guys on the team. Except for Jabril. Jabril was as rock solid as ever. He could be Gabe's friend and Alex's at the same time. The only thing that had changed since the start of the football season was that Alex and Jabril were closer than they'd ever been. Whatever lost time she had with Gabe, it was like she was making it up with Jabril.

She had a good practice Tuesday night. They all did, getting ready for their next home game against the team from Seneca. It was the first time Alex thought she might have gotten as many snaps with the first-team offense as Jeff Stiles did. Lewis Healey's ankle sprain was healed, and he was back to practicing at full speed. But it was clear that Coach Mencken no longer saw Lewis as an option for backup quarterback. For now, that was Alex's job. They'd played two games, and she'd gotten to play in each one.

Another surprise of the football season?

She seemed to be winning over her coach.

It gave her hope. Maybe if he could get past her—what, her girl-ness?—maybe the rest of the team would follow. Eventually.

But every time she allowed herself to hope, something else would happen. Tonight it came at the end of practice, Alex out there with the first team, Coach giving her one last chance to get a score. Like it was fourth down at the end of a game.

The offense was at the twelve-yard line. Coach was letting Alex call her own play. She called a pass to Lewis, since she'd made no secret that she preferred throwing the ball to Gabe. In the huddle, Alex didn't call one of their set plays. She just told Lewis to run for the end zone, make a quick break to the outside, and get open. She'd handle the rest.

Alex dropped back and was given plenty of time by her blockers, mostly due to Cal putting a perfect block on a blitzing Jabril. She gave a quick glance to her left—looking the defenders off, the way pro quarterbacks did—then turned to Lewis, who was making his break.

To the inside.

Not the outside.

Her pass sailed out of bounds.

Practice over.

She'd told him where to go. Couldn't have been any clearer. The guys in the huddle had heard her, too. But she didn't make a thing out of it in front of the team. She knew better, and besides, she had enough trouble with Lewis Healey as it was.

He was walking back to the bench when she came up along-side him.

"What was that?" she said, keeping her voice low.

He already had his helmet off and carried it in his hand. Turning to her with a smirk on his face that Alex thought was permanently there, he shrugged and said, "Oops."

"You know I said to break to the outside."

"I heard inside," he said, continuing to stare straight ahead.

Alex stopped and planted herself in front of him, blocking his way. "No, you didn't."

"Calling me a liar?" he said. "Because if you are, say what you have to say in front of the whole team."

"You'd like that," Alex said.

"Man up," Lewis said.

And walked away.

"You should quit," Sophie said.

They were at Alex's house the next day after school, Wednesday. Kelly was downstairs in the kitchen doing homework, which is what she usually did when she came to the house to watch Alex. Alex and Sophie were on the swing set in her backyard. The one her dad had assembled for her as a birthday gift when she was six and refused to take down.

Alex had debated whether to tell Sophie what had happened with Lewis Healey the night before. She didn't want Sophie to think she went running to her every time somebody on the team tried to hurt her feelings.

Or did.

But right now the only person other than Sophie in whom she could confide was Jabril. And as good a guy as Jabril was, he was still a guy. Even so, he would never have suggested she quit.

But that's exactly what Sophie was telling her now, much to Alex's surprise.

"Wait, *what*?" Alex said.

They had been swinging pretty high, but now Alex kicked her feet to the ground to slow herself.

"You've been my biggest cheerleader up to now," Alex said.

"I see what you did there," Sophie said.

"And now you're the one telling me to quit?"

"I'll tell you why," Sophie said. "This is supposed to be fun for you, even with all the junk you've had to put up with."

"*Lots* of junk."

"And I know it's a lot. But sports are supposed to be fun. If cheerleading made me as miserable as football makes you, I'm pretty sure *I'd* quit, too."

"But your teammates want you on your team."

"Listen," Sophie said. "I won't pretend cheerleading is always sunshine and rainbows. There are times when it's really tough. The hours are long, people get hurt, my teammates don't agree on stuff, and we argue a lot. I mean, *a lot*. But at the end of the day, we're all passionate about the same thing."

"I just feel like the guys are never going to see it from my point of view," Alex said. "Like, there's no light at the end of the tunnel. I'm going to be dealing with this for as long as I want to play football, and it's not fair!"

The last sentence came out in hot anger. Louder than she'd

intended, and not meant to be aimed at Sophie. She quickly apologized, but Sophie shook her head.

"Don't apologize for being upset," she said. "You're allowed to feel this way. And I'm sorry something you love is tied up and tangled with all this hate. It shouldn't be like that."

Alex could feel the frustration boiling up in her, so she inhaled deep and let it out through her nose.

"But you're wrong," Sophie said. "There is a bright side. Like anything else, after a while the guys are going to get bored and move on to something more interesting. The novelty of a girl on the team won't be the hot new scandal anymore."

"I know," Alex said, head hanging between her legs. "But that might take a while in Orville, Pennsylvania."

Sophie laughed. "Is your coach doing anything to shut them up?"

"Who, the guys?" Alex said.

Sophie rolled her eyes back, as if to say, *Who else?*

"Not as much as he could be," Alex admitted. Thinking it would be nice to have the full support of an authority figure, and not have to always fly solo. She also couldn't forget that Coach was originally opposed to having Alex on the team. He was slowly coming around, but at this point, she couldn't consider him a true ally. Not yet.

Sophie listened. Then shrugged. "It's not an ideal solution, but if you ignore the teasing and resist their jabs, they're going to back off. And honestly? It's not exactly in their best interest to purposely mess up plays. In the end, they all want to win."

"I try not to let them get to me," Alex said.

"Block out the negativity as best you can."

"I guess in order to be QB I have to learn to block things out," Alex said.

"That's the spirit!" Sophie said, leaping up from her swing.

Alex got up, too, and decided to thank Sophie in her own way.

"You mean . . . I got spirit, yes, I do, I got spirit, how 'bout you?" she said, perfectly clasping her hands like the cheerleaders did. It was a cheer she'd heard on the sidelines during games.

Sophie doubled over laughing. "Yes!!" she yelled. "You got it!"

"See, I can still be fun."

"Now you're your own cheerleader," Sophie said. "And you just gave me a brilliant idea."

Sophie asked Alex to grab her football from inside. Alex was happy to oblige, even if she was a little curious what Sophie had up her sleeve.

"Okay," Alex said, ball in hand, "you want to start with some pass drills?"

Sophie shook her head. "First, you're going to learn a proper cheer."

"Uhh, excuse me?" Alex said. "Did I not just perform one two minutes ago?"

Sophie snorted, "Ha! Please. That was just a chant."

Clearly there was a lot Alex didn't know about cheerleading.

"Okay, well, I'm just letting you know now?" Alex said, tossing the ball to the side. "This won't end well."

They stood in the middle of the yard as Sophie began to show Alex some basic cheerleading moves. Apparently, there was even a right and wrong way to clap.

"Okay, back to basics," Sophie said, and had Alex face her. "Do what I do."

She put her arms at her sides, then bent them at the elbows and cupped her hands together in front of her face. "This is called a clasp."

"I don't see how anybody could call this clapping," Alex said. "Or clasping. Or whatever."

"You know what it really is?" Sophie said happily. *"Cheerleading."*

"For the record," Alex said, "after today, I'm never doing this again."

"Fair enough," said Sophie.

They went through other moves. One was called a high *V*. Tight fists. Arms in the air forming a perfect letter *V*.

"And I assume you know how to signal for a touchdown, right?" Sophie said to Alex.

"Well, *yeah*," Alex said, showing her, with arms out, elbows bent, and hands up.

"Now we do some jumps," Sophie said.

"We're not done yet?" Alex complained.

"Come on," Sophie said. "That was just a warm-up."

She demonstrated the correct approach for what was called a toe-touch. You started with a high *V*, then swooped your arms down into a squat before using the force to pull up and jump, touching your toes on either side. The key, Sophie said, was to land with your feet close together.

"Like sticking the finish in gymnastics," Sophie said, after illustrating what the jump should look like. Sophie's legs went into an almost perfect split in the air. Alex had to admit, she was impressed.

The first time Alex tried that one, she landed on her butt. And the second time. And the third. She was determined, though, to get the hang of it. Sophie made her do it a few times in a row, just to prove she had it down.

After about a hundred jumps, or so it seemed to Alex, she tumbled to the ground in exhaustion.

"Aw, don't tell me you're tired!" Sophie said, still full of pep.

"You weren't the one doing all the jumps!" Alex laughed, breathing heavy.

Sophie replied, "That's because I do this every *day*. Now get up. Time to move on to the hard ones."

"Wait," Alex said, catching her breath. "These were the easy ones?"

Sophie rolled her eyes and pulled Alex up off the ground.

"I'm tired," Alex moaned.

"Is that what you say to Coach Mencken?" Sophie said.

Alex made a sound that was half sigh, half groan. "What now?" she said.

Sophie showed Alex the pike jump and the tuck jump and a side hurdler, which Alex found the most difficult of all.

Once Alex was all cheered out for the day, she said to Sophie, "Okay, now it's my turn."

She reached down to grab the football and taught Sophie how to grip it, with her fingers lining up with the laces. Alex went long and had Sophie throw her a few passes. She actually had a pretty decent arm.

"The result of lifting people over my head on a daily basis," Sophie said, squeezing her biceps.

Alex showed Sophie how to put a spin on the ball and even how to hike it to Alex. They went through drills and patterns. Alex had Sophie running all over the backyard.

"Most I've run since cheer tryouts," Sophie said, panting.

Alex laughed. "This is what we call payback."

When they were done for the day, hair a mess, dirty and aching, Sophie bumped Alex in the hip.

"So?" she said. "Did you have fun, despite yourself?"

"Gotta admit," Alex said, "I did."

"You know what I think is the best move for you?" Sophie said.

"What's that?"

"Getting out of your own way."

THEIR THIRD GAME WAS AGAINST THE SENECA BEARS, AND THEY were off to a rough start. The Bears were ahead by a touchdown by the middle of the second quarter. Jeff had already thrown an interception and fumbled in the pocket when he didn't see the pressure coming from behind him.

During a change-of-possession time-out, when the Owls had the ball back, Coach told Alex he was putting her in. Then he walked over and told Jeff he was coming out.

"It's only the second quarter!" Jeff said in a voice that Alex thought was loud enough that the parents and fans in the bleachers could hear.

Coach leaned down and said something quietly in his ear. Alex saw Jeff shaking his head.

"*I'm* the quarterback of this team," Jeff said, pumping a fist to his chest.

Alex moved a little closer, trying to hear Coach's side of the conversation.

"We have two quarterbacks on our team, son," Coach Mencken said.

"Yeah, and one's *a girl!*"

He said it in what Alex could only describe as a growl. Like it had been pent up inside him, waiting to burst out.

Alex thought Jeff was way out of line, talking back to Coach like that. But Coach was keeping his composure. Alex wondered if Coach was being easy on him to soften the blow of getting pulled out of the game. Unfortunately, Jeff wasn't done with his little temper tantrum.

"You honestly think *she's* a better quarterback?" Jeff yelled, pointing at Alex. "You think she'll give us a better chance to win the game?"

"Maybe today," Coach said. Though to Alex, he sounded more curt than before. Like he was losing patience with Jeff.

Right then, the ref blew his whistle and was waving the Owls back onto the field.

Coach held up a finger to Jeff. "Now I'd appreciate it if you'd not say another word to me right now. And you better start supporting your teammates." He paused. *"All* of your teammates."

Jeff stood there frozen a moment longer. Whatever he had left to say would remain unsaid. Then he walked away from Coach and down the sideline until he was standing alone at the Owls' thirty-yard line.

Coach waved Alex over and gave her the first three plays he wanted to run. A handoff to Tariq. Slant pass to Gabe. Then an option play, where Alex could either pitch the ball to Tariq or keep it herself.

The Owls already had one loss. Maybe they could survive another and still make it to the championship game. Of course, nobody on the team wanted to find out.

"What we need," Coach said, "is a couple of first downs."

The Owls were starting the drive at their own twenty-yard

line. On first down, Tariq gained twelve yards, running behind Perry Moses through a huge hole and up the middle. On the next play Alex got some pressure but had time to get the ball cleanly to Gabe, who gained ten yards and another first down.

On the option play, Alex noticed the defenders were cheating toward Tariq, sure that Alex was planning to pitch him the ball. So she kept it instead, cutting to the inside. Then *she* gained ten yards on the play.

Just like that, they were past midfield.

Jake Caldwell came in for the next play. Alex came to meet him, then knelt down in the huddle. Hunched over in the circle, her teammates surrounding her, Alex noticed something. There was no chatter now. She was the only one talking, calling the play. She had their attention. They could all feel the game changing a little bit.

She wasn't the girl quarterback right now.

Just the quarterback.

The call was a swing pass in the flat to Tariq. When he caught it, it was as though the whole Owls team was in front of him, blocking. He finally ran twenty yards before getting shoved out of bounds.

They were inside the Bears' thirty-yard line now.

The next play Coach sent in was for Gabe. Coach must have sensed the same shift in the game as his players. They had the Bears backing up. TV commentators talked about guys running downhill, and that's the way the game felt now. Coach decided to go for it, calling one of Gabe's favorite patterns: a fake to the inside and then a deep cut toward the corner of the end zone.

Alex had all the time in the world to set herself in the pocket, then wait for Gabe to make his cut and—hopefully—be open when he did.

He was.

Alex put just enough air under her throw, dropping it over the safety scrambling to catch up to Gabe just as Gabe crossed into the end zone.

The Owls were on the board. Then Tariq ran the ball in for the conversion.

Now they were ahead, 7–6.

As Alex ran off the field, she noticed Gabe running to catch up with her, probably to say something about the touchdown play.

"Nice throw," he said.

"Nice catch," she replied.

It wasn't much.

But it was something.

It was still Owls 7, Bears 6 at halftime. But that wasn't the news, at least not to Alex. The news was that she was staying in the game to start the second half.

They'd had a couple of promising drives at the end of the second quarter that stalled after her touchdown pass to Gabe. Tariq had fumbled, and Alex had a pass tipped by one of the Bears' defensive linemen, which was intercepted by their middle linebacker after they'd gotten back inside the Bears' twenty-yard line.

But they'd clearly moved the ball better with her in there. So Coach let her stay in there.

"Girl," Jabril whispered as the two teams lined up for the

kickoff, "might be the second half. But you're looking first string to me."

Alex beamed.

"Now don't screw it up," he said.

"That's your pep talk?" she said.

"Tough love," he said, giving her a wink from behind his facemask.

Once again Coach scripted the first three plays for her. Quick sideline pass to Lewis. Straight handoff to Tariq. But Alex over-threw Lewis, and Tariq only got two yards during his play. So it was third-and-eight.

The call was to Gabe again, a post pattern deep down the middle.

"Gonna need some time," Alex said to the guys in the offensive line.

"You got it," Cal said.

They gave her the time. Gabe beat his man and got behind the safeties. Then, as if she and Gabe were the only two on the field, Alex gunned the ball in his direction. Gabe didn't have to break stride, catching it easily in his gloved hands. Then he was in the clear, veering toward the sideline and running toward the end zone.

Now it was 13–6, Owls. Sophie and the rest of the cheerleaders were positioned at that end of the field. As Gabe crossed the goal line, Alex saw a blur of high *V*s and toe-touches and clasps. Sophie picked up the megaphone beside her and shouted into it, "Way to go, Alex!!"

Alex locked eyes with Sophie from across the field and saw

her do a high kick while shaking her poms in the air. A special cheer for only Alex.

Afterward, Jake dropped the conversion pass, so the score remained 13–6.

For the second time that night, Alex and Gabe ran off the field together.

"Nice throw," he said again.

Alex couldn't help herself.

"I *know*," she said.

Gabe shook his head, but Alex could swear she saw him smiling. He ran ahead of her, passing Jabril, who'd come out onto the field to slap Alex a high five so enthusiastic it nearly knocked her to the ground.

"Hey," Alex said. "I'm on your side, remember?"

She was getting a drink of water at the cooler when she heard a voice behind her.

"Have your fun while you can."

She didn't have to turn around to know it was Jeff Stiles. Even with their team ahead, this was his idea of being a good teammate.

"Excuse me?" Alex said.

She'd heard him perfectly the first time but wanted him to repeat it to her face.

"I said that you should have your fun while you can," he said, louder this time.

Remembering what Sophie had told her about not playing into their nonsense, Alex tipped back her helmet and gave Jeff the biggest smile she could muster.

"Okay," she said, and walked away.

The Owls quickly realized the game was far from over. On one of their best drives of the game, the Bears returned the Owls' punt, taking the ball down the field for a touchdown. It was 13–12. But on the conversion attempt Jabril was somehow able to travel from one side of the end zone to the other, to knock down a pass attempt to their tight end, keeping the Owls ahead by a point.

One point. And just under two minutes to go, with the ball on their forty-one-yard line.

"They've got two time-outs left," Coach said to Alex. "We get one first down and this baby is over."

"Got it," she said.

"Hand it to Tariq the first two downs," he said. "Protect the ball and tell him the same thing. We'll see where we are if we *don't* have the first down by then."

Alex nodded. She started to run out to the huddle, but Coach stopped her by placing a hand on her arm.

"Go win the game," he said, a silent message passing between them. Alex knew his perspective of her had changed since the beginning of the season. Coach had faith in her, just like she had faith in herself.

She sprinted to join her teammates. This wasn't the fourth quarter of a blowout game. This was a one-point game. One they needed to close out and win.

This was football.

People kept asking her why.

This was why.

She told the guys the play and the snap count. They began to turn toward the line of scrimmage.

"Hey?" Alex said.

They turned back around.

"Do your jobs," she said.

Where did that come from?

She knew it was something Coach Bill Belichick told his players all the time. Now she got to say it to the Orville Owls.

She felt herself smiling as she got ready to do her job.

But the Bears stacked the line and stopped Tariq for no gain. They called their first time-out. On second down, Tariq got just three yards before they stuffed him again.

The Bears called their last time-out with a minute and forty seconds left.

Third-and-seven.

If they got the first down here, the Bears couldn't stop the ball again. If they didn't, they'd have to punt, and the Bears would get the ball back with around a minute left. Still enough time to make a big play and win the game themselves.

Jake brought in the play from the sideline.

A pass play. To Gabe. Over the middle.

"He wants me to try a throw?" Alex said, knowing an incompletion would stop the clock and give the Bears even more time when they got the ball back.

She didn't even allow herself to think what another interception would mean, even though she'd thrown one today already.

She saw Jake grin.

"No," he said. "Coach wants you to *make* a throw."

She quieted her mind, telling herself not to think about what might go wrong.

Make a throw.

Win the game, like Coach had told her to.

This time it was Gabe who quietly said, "We got this."

The Bears blitzed. They came up the middle and from both sides of the line. Alex had no time to get the ball to Gabe, no choice but to run out of the pocket, away from the pressure. There was space to her left. If she could find Gabe, it was going to be harder to make a throw as a right-hander running on the left. Alex knew she could do it, though. *If* she could get it to him.

Before the defense got to her.

She caught a glimpse of Gabe running back in her direction from where he'd been in the middle of the field.

Truth or dare, Alex thought.

Run or pass.

The girl her dad had dubbed a triple threat decided she had to run for the first down. The pass was too risky, and she was nearly out of time.

Get around the corner, get to the first-down marker.

Win the game.

She faked a throw and pulled the ball down, looking ahead to see one Bears player between her and the marker. It was one of their linebackers. No. 53. He'd been in her face plenty of times today. Now there he was again.

Until he wasn't.

Gabe had flown in from the guy's left, clearing him out with a perfect, clean, and legal block.

Alex not only got past the marker, she wasn't even forced to run out of bounds as more defenders came for her. She simply went into her slide.

First down.

Ball game.

Football.

Yeah.

This was why.

She *was* going to enjoy it for as long as she possibly could.

27

Alex and Sophie made a plan to meet for ice cream that afternoon. Sophie's grandparents were in town, so she was eating lunch at home.

"Leave room for ice cream," Alex said.

"There's *always* room for ice cream," Sophie said.

Alex's dad took her to lunch at their local diner. He planned to drop her in town to meet Sophie while he went to the hardware store to pick up a few things.

"What kind of things?" Alex said.

"Fix-it-type things," he said.

"Dad," she said. "I thought we agreed that fix-it-type things weren't really *your* thing."

"It's Saturday," he said. "I just feel like the hardware store is somewhere I should be."

Alex laughed. "Just don't try to fix anything in my room," she said. "Remember what happened last time?"

They both knew she meant the time he hammered his own finger trying to hang a shelf on her wall. His nail never grew back the same.

Now he smiled at her across the table.

"You were great today," he said.

She shook her head.

"No?" he said.

"I wasn't great," she said. "But I was very *good*."

"Fun, right?" he said.

"Sophie told me I better start having fun again," she said. "Or it won't be worth it."

"Maybe that's a sort of fix-it project for you," her dad said.

"Unfortunately, nothing at the hardware store can help with that."

"You sure you don't want to come and hang with me before you meet Sophie?"

Alex shrugged. "Kind of going to make that my last pass of the day," she said.

Jack parked at the hardware store. It was a pretty small town, so Alex's dad let her roam by herself, within reason. Taylor Books was adjacent to the hardware store, and Bostwick's was across the street. Alex told her dad she was going to stop at the bookstore before meeting Sophie. Being surrounded by books made her feel smarter, somehow, even without having to open them. Though, of course, she did open them. Especially books about football. Right now, she was reading a nonfiction book about Jim Thorpe, a Native American athlete.

Jim Thorpe inspired her because he was the first Native American to win a gold medal for the United States. The first. She knew she wasn't the first girl to ever join a football team. There were other women she'd read about. High school and college-age players who fought to play. But reading and hearing about their stories seemed so far away from Orville, Pennsylvania, and the Owls football team. Though they did encourage her to keep going and keep fighting.

She was still on cloud nine. She'd made a play to win the game. It wasn't the only play that had helped the Owls come out on top, and it wasn't the one Coach called. When it was all on the line, Alex had called her own number.

But the high she felt wasn't just from the game. It was also from what Coach Mencken said to her afterward.

He'd pulled her aside, walking away from her teammates.

"Something I need to tell you," he said.

Alex's stomach coiled in knots. She thought she'd just done something good for her team. But it was like she was trained to expect bad news. She looked up at Coach, waiting for him to continue.

"I'll be the first to admit, I didn't think you could do this." He paused. "But you can."

Alex's shoulders relaxed. "Thank you."

"And I hate to say it, but I didn't want you on this team," he said.

"Had a feeling," she said, "even if you didn't come right out and say it like the other guys."

"You deserve an apology," he said. "I was wrong. Dead wrong. And I'm sorry. I hope the guys on the team come around, and I'll do whatever I can to help make that happen."

"Thanks, Coach," Alex said. There was nothing else she could say. It was more than she could have hoped for. Having Coach in her corner was all she needed. Even if the others never grew to accept her.

A permanent smile had been plastered on her face ever since. But it began to fall when Alex spotted Annie Burgess coming into the bookstore, still dressed in her soccer uniform. Alex knew the girls' soccer team had a game this morning against Valley Falls.

Last season, Annie, a center back on defense and one of the team captains, had been Alex's best friend on the team. But so far at school, they'd hardly spoken. Alex just assumed she was on Team Jeff.

Alex thought the whole idea of there being a Team Jeff vs. Team Alex was as dumb as a bag of hammers, to borrow a phrase from her dad.

There was, she knew, no way to avoid Annie.

Or vice versa.

"Hey," Alex said.

"Hey," was Annie's abrupt reply.

Already it was awkward, but nothing Alex wasn't accustomed to. Other than Jabril and Sophie, there wasn't anyone in the entire seventh grade who wasn't awkward toward her these days.

"You guys win?" Alex said.

"Yeah," Annie said. "What about you?"

"Squeaked one out."

"Did you get to play?"

"Played most of the game," Alex said. "Surprisingly."

They were keeping to small talk. But at least they were talking.

"Did you play well?" Annie asked.

Alex wasn't sure how to answer that, especially with so many of her classmates thinking she was stuck on herself. But she *had* played well. And she was allowed to say that.

"I did," she said. "Got lucky and made a big run at the end to kind of clinch things for us. What about you?"

Annie didn't hesitate.

"I moved up and scored a goal," she said, a grin forming. "First one since last season."

"Annie, that's amazing!" Alex said. "I always thought you'd be one of our best scorers if you played up front. Coach kept you back because you're the best defender we have."

"Sounds like you're still on the team," Annie said, her expression transitioning to one that was both sad and annoyed. "Only you're not."

"C'mon, Annie," Alex said. "You know me. You know I'm still rooting for you guys."

"Then why did you quit?" It was the question she was expecting, but it still felt like a punch to the gut.

The question hung in the air between them. Suddenly, Alex felt as if Annie was back on offense.

"I quit to try something else," Alex said, a little tired of having to explain herself.

"What's wrong with soccer?" Annie said.

"Nothing!" said Alex. "But haven't you ever wanted to see if you could be great at something else?"

Annie shuffled uncomfortably, shifting her weight from foot to foot.

"I didn't *do* anything to the team," Alex continued. "I just did this for myself. Can't anybody understand that?"

"We—I mean, the other girls and I—think we could have won the regional championship if you'd stayed on the team. Now we might not."

"I wasn't that good!" Alex said, surprised at how hot the words came out.

"You made us better," Annie said. It was a compliment, but it didn't come out like one.

"You guys are still good enough without me," Alex said. "I know that, and I haven't even seen you play yet."

Annie glanced past Alex, as if looking for a way out of the conversation. But she didn't walk away.

"There's just been a lot of talk about you," she said.

"Let me guess," Alex said. "Most of it is from Lindsey Stiles."

Annie said, "Well, yeah. She and Jeff are stirring the pot."

"Why Lindsey cares, I have no idea," Alex said. "It's not like she and I had much to do with each other even when I *was* on the team."

"She just thinks it's wrong that you're trying to take Jeff's job," Annie said. "And that you didn't even have to do this."

Doing more than *trying*, Alex thought. It gave her a brief rush of optimism.

"All I'm doing is what you did today in soccer: competing. You were given a chance at another position today, and you were great. Why shouldn't I have that same opportunity?"

Annie shook her head. "Not the same."

"It's exactly the same," Alex said. "And as soon as you all accept that, we can finally move on with our lives."

All the frustration had finally come to a head, and Alex was relieved to say out loud what she'd been thinking all along. It was time everyone got over themselves.

"I have to go," Annie said.

"So that's it?" Alex said. "I thought we were friends."

"We are," Annie said. "Just not right now."

Alex shook her head. "Being somebody's friend isn't a part-time job."

Annie started past her, but Alex took a step to block her way.

"Do me a favor," Alex said. "When you see Lindsey, tell her she was wrong. I *did* have to do this."

Then Annie was past her and gone, out the front door and walking quickly up Main Street, away from Alex. The center back on Team Jeff.

28

THE OWLS WON THEIR NEXT TWO GAMES. IN THE FIRST ONE, JEFF got more snaps than Alex and managed to complete more passes than he had in any game all season.

He kept telling kids at school, spreading the word that he deserved to be the quarterback. Alex thought that for once he'd lived up to all his big talk.

In the second game, against the Camden Heights Vikings, Jeff had a terrible first quarter and Coach took him out early. At least the game was still scoreless when he did. Jabril was to thank for that, along with the rest of the defensive line.

Just like when they'd played the Bears, the game took a turn for the Owls' offense as soon as Alex took the field. Whatever the guys thought about her being on the team, whatever they were saying behind her back, it was clear they responded to her presence behind center. Jabril told her that a lot of the guys privately admitted they knew she was better than Jeff. Why they couldn't say it out loud was a mystery to Alex. It's not like Jeff was the king of England.

"Which guys think that?" Alex had asked, curious who among them might be turning a corner.

"Can't tell you," he said. "Promised I wouldn't." He shot Alex a prize-winning grin. It was like Sophie's, in that seeing it suddenly made Alex feel better about everything. "I know how to be a good teammate even if some of my brothers still haven't figured that out."

"I'm a good teammate, right?" Alex said, elbowing him in the side.

"As good as you are a QB," he said.

She showed how good a QB she was against the Vikings right away. The team went on a long drive that resulted in a touchdown run from Tariq, followed by an even longer drive in the third quarter that ended with Alex completing a pass to Lewis Healey for his first touchdown of the season. She didn't say anything to him after his catch and run, and he didn't say anything to her. Not even when they got back to the sideline. By then, he was trying to disguise his happiness in front of his pal Jeff.

But Alex knew the truth about the wide receivers, even the ones who didn't like her: they really didn't care who was getting them the ball as long as *somebody* was.

The Owls won, 13–0, extending their record to 4-1. As usual, Jabril was everywhere on defense, making tackles, forcing turnovers, making the Vikings' quarterback probably wish he'd chosen another fall sport.

Coach pulled her aside for another private chat once the game ended. Their chats never lasted long, but he seemed to enjoy them. So did Alex. It was just another way football was surprising her recently.

It seemed to Alex that Coach Mencken had gone from tolerating, to accepting, to actually favoring her as a player.

"Between us?" he said.

Alex nodded.

"I know you want to start," he said, "just because who wouldn't?"

"My dad always said it doesn't matter who's out there to start the game as much as who's out there to finish it," she said.

"Maybe so," he said. "But I feel it's my responsibility to explain why you're not starting. Our team is going good with the way we're doing things. We seem to have found our stride. I just don't want to mess with success."

"I don't want to either," Alex said.

He nodded. Might even have smiled. Alex wasn't sure.

"Good game today," he said. "But you're a smart kid, so you probably knew that already."

To Alex's disappointment, Jabril and his dad had already left. He was the only teammate who usually stuck around to celebrate with Alex while the rest of the team drifted off to the locker room. She searched for Gabe, thinking maybe they could talk about the game now that no one was around. But he was gone, too.

Sophie, though, was waiting for her near the bleachers with Jack Carlisle, both with looks on their faces that said they knew something she didn't.

"What?" she said, her eyes flitting from Sophie to her dad.

At which point her goofball dad struck one of Sophie's cheerleader poses, arms straight down at his sides, before going into the clasp.

"Oh god," Alex said. "Stop before somebody else sees."

"Sophie taught me the vault. Wanna see?"

"Please don't," Alex said, shielding her eyes.

"You know, he's actually not bad," Sophie said.

"I'm begging you both," Alex said, this time backing up, like the embarrassment was too much.

"I'll go get the car," her dad said, to Alex's relief.

Sophie sidled up to Alex and wrapped an arm around her shoulder.

"Hey, girl," she said. "How we lookin'?"

"Still a long way to go," Alex said.

"You're allowed to celebrate the wins, you know."

"Well, the wins won't matter unless we make it to the championship," Alex said.

"Not talking about games," said Sophie. "You've come a long way since tryouts. Take some time to recognize that."

Alex knew she was right. Just like she knew how lucky she was to have a friend like Sophie.

"Good point," she said.

With that, they walked off the field together.

The Steelers had been on the road the past couple of Sundays. But they were back at Heinz Field this week to play the Baltimore Ravens.

This time Alex had more reason to be excited than she usually was for a season game. Despite the fact that he didn't play for the Steelers, Lamar Jackson, the quarterback for the Ravens, was her favorite player on the planet. The only reason she didn't have a poster of him on her bedroom wall was because she thought it would be disloyal to her team.

Because the Steelers and Ravens were in the same division,

she got to see Lamar Jackson in person once a year. This was the Sunday she always circled on her Steelers calendar. Now it was here.

She loved watching Lamar play. Alex's dad said he was the fastest guy to ever play quarterback in the NFL, and Alex was sure he was right. She couldn't imagine anybody being faster. But it was more than that. Alex had followed him in college and knew that while he'd won the Heisman Trophy, people wondered if he could throw well enough to be the same kind of star in the pros that he'd been when he played for Louisville. Alex remembered one guy on ESPN saying that the Ravens should think about turning him into a wide receiver. She immediately changed the channel. She didn't think he was just going to be good for the Ravens.

She thought he was going to be great. And once he got *his* chance to get on the field, during his rookie season, he proved her right. He made all the throws and made up plays when being chased. The way he played made it seem effortless.

"You know what the best thing about him is?" Alex's dad said when they found their seats before kickoff. "He blocked out all the noise. He ignored the doubters. And it made him stronger and more determined to prove them all wrong."

She poked him with an elbow. "I get it, Dad," she said.

"Get what?" he said. "Just making an observation."

"So you're saying I'm the Lamar of seventh-grade football?" she said.

"How are all the ones who doubted you looking right now?"

"Long way to go," she said.

He scratched his head and said, "I could swear I've heard that one before."

The Steelers lost to the Ravens. Or, more accurately, they lost to Lamar Jackson. He ended up throwing for more than three hundred yards, and he ran for a hundred more, throwing one touchdown pass and running for another.

He did all that. He *was* all that.

On the way home Alex said to her dad, "I wish my teammates loved me the way the Ravens love Lamar."

"They'll come around."

"You really believe that?" Alex said. "We've already played more than half the season."

"I'll level with you," her dad said. "If a girl had made my team in high school, I probably would have initially reacted the same way as your teammates."

"Because you would've thought a girl shouldn't be playing with boys?"

"No," he said. "I just think everybody is resistant to change, at least at first. But pretty soon they'll realize you're there for the same reason they are: to play. You're on common ground."

"So you would have gotten over it—is that what you're saying?" Alex said.

"Part of maturing is becoming more open-minded," he said. "The boys on your team have only ever known one way of playing football: without girls. Now that they're playing with a girl, it'll broaden their horizons a bit. "

"Put me down as a doubter on that," Alex said.

"One more person you'll have to prove wrong," Jack Carlisle said to his daughter.

IN HER ROOM LATER THAT EVENING, ALEX DID THE LAST OF HER homework, then read a few more pages of the Aaron Rodgers biography her dad bought her. He was her original favorite quarterback, before Lamar Jackson came on the scene.

She'd smiled when she found her clean jersey and football pants neatly folded on her desk chair. When it came to laundry, Jack Carlisle didn't mess around.

She was lying on the bed with Simba beside her. Just another reminder of how far she'd come since that day at the fair. At the time, she'd thought her three chances at the carnival game would be the only throws she'd get to make all year.

Or ever.

And that Simba would be the only football prize she'd ever win.

But now she was a quarterback on the Orville Owls, trying to win games and setting her sights on a much bigger prize: the league's championship trophy.

"Sophie's right," Alex said to her lion. "We *have* come a long way, you and me."

She still didn't feel like part of the team the way you were supposed to. And that made her sad sometimes. Made her miss soccer, too, and almost regret quitting the team. Almost. She was the girl who'd done this because she'd wanted to prove that she could be great at something, better than she'd ever been at anything else. But she'd also wanted to be a part of something bigger than herself.

Maybe her mom was right.

Maybe you didn't always get it all, no matter how much you wanted it. There would always be a stumbling block in the way.

But those blocks were fewer now. Every time she gave out the play in the huddle, or took it upon herself to *make* a play, the other guys saw what she was made of. They had to acknowledge her as part of the team.

When she was out there, she loved being a football player more than she ever thought she would.

It might not have turned out exactly the way she'd imagined. But for now, it would have to be enough. Because her heart was set on a much bigger prize: the championship. She wanted that in football more than in any other sport. And soon it became clear to her why. After all the hurdles she'd had to overcome just to be on the team, winning the championship would be like icing on the cake. The climax of her story. Like reaching the top of a mountain. She wanted to be out there, hoisting the championship trophy high in the air, surrounded by her teammates—the ones who accepted her and the ones who didn't.

"It doesn't mean I don't think you were a prize, Simba," she whispered in her room. "I'm just looking for one more."

Then she rolled her eyes. *I'm talking to a stuffed animal.*

She hugged him tight to her chest. Some of her friends might say that stuffed animals were too babyish for a seventh grader. But Alex didn't care. They comforted her. And comfort was what she needed right now.

Ordinarily, Alex put her phone on silent when she was studying or reading. But she'd forgotten tonight and heard a faint buzzing now, coming from her nightstand. She reached over and grabbed her phone, checking the screen.

Mom.

She'd made sure to call after every one of Alex's games, whether they took place on Saturdays or Sundays.

"Hey, Mama," Alex said.

"Hey, you," her mom said. "I just spent about seventeen hours straight at the hospital and didn't get the chance to call yesterday. Did we win or lose?"

"Won."

"How'd you do?"

"Really well," Alex said.

"No surprise there," her mom said. "How much did you get to play?"

"A lot," Alex said. "From the second quarter on."

She told her mom what Coach said about not wanting to mess with success.

"Sounds like the success is you, hon," her mom said. "Of course, I don't know a lot about sports."

"Oh, I think we've established that," Alex said.

She heard her mom giggle. The more they had these postgame calls, the closer Alex felt to her. Not as close as some mothers and daughters, but one step at a time. Right now, her mom was like the big sister Alex never had.

"But even though I am no expert," her mom said, "it seems to me that if you're the best quarterback on the team, you're the one who should be starting."

"It's not that big a deal to me," Alex said. But even as the words left her mouth, she knew they were a lie.

"Are you sure about that?"

"Mom, it's not like I could change Coach's mind even if I tried," she said. "Which I refuse to do."

"Okaaaay," her mom said in singsong, "but I bet there isn't another position where the best person for the job isn't the one starting."

"So you think it's because I'm a girl."

"I don't think. I know."

"You're not even here," Alex said.

It came out harsher than she'd meant. It sounded like criticism even if all she was doing was stating a fact.

Long pause now from her mom's end of the call.

"I know I'm not," she said finally.

"I didn't mean it to sound like a bad thing," Alex said. "I promise. It's just—"

"You don't have to apologize for anything," her mom said. "You're my hero for doing this. And I want you to know that even though I'm not there, I'm still *here* for you. I'm just frustrated that my daughter has to suffer through the same double standards as I did all those years ago."

"I know," Alex said. "But all I can do is keep my head down and continue doing what I'm doing."

"I hear you," her mom said. "You've rocked their world. You don't want to rock the boat."

"Okay," Alex said. "Enough rocking for one night."

"Roger that."

"Hey, at least I've got the coach on my side," Alex said. "I sure didn't see *that* coming."

"Well, he wants to win, doesn't he?" Dr. Liza Borelli said. "Remind your father to send me some video. I think he forgot yesterday."

Alex said she would.

"How are things going with your friend Gabe, by the way?"

"Great on the field," Alex said. "But nothing's changed between us off it."

"So he's still being a wimpball."

"He's not a wimpball," Alex said. "Which isn't even a word, pretty sure."

"I know, I just made it up," her mom said.

"He's a good guy," Alex said. "He didn't sign up for being in the middle of all this."

"So you're not mad at him?"

"Not mad," Alex said. "Maybe a little disappointed. But definitely not mad."

Just then, Alex heard some voices in the background through the phone.

"Gotta go, babe. But I love you," Alex's mom said. "Whether I'm there or not."

"I know," Alex said. "Love you, too."

She pressed END on her phone and plunked down in her desk chair. A framed photo of her and her mom sat on her window ledge. It was from when her mom had come to visit last fall. They were standing on a dock at Orville Lake, her mom with an arm wrapped around Alex's shoulder, the multicolored leaves peppering the background.

They were both smiling.

Alex stared at the picture.

"Here for me," she said to Simba. "But definitely *not* here."

30

THE REGULAR SEASON WAS SET TO END TWO SATURDAYS BEFORE Thanksgiving. If the Owls made the championship game, it would be scheduled for the Saturday after that, at the home field of the team with the best record in the league.

Three games left. Three teams tied with one loss. The Owls were one of them. The others—Carrolton and Washington Falls—were still on the schedule, so the Owls could either knock them both out or get knocked out themselves. To Alex, it felt as if the playoffs had already begun.

October now in Orville. Football weather almost every single day in western Pennsylvania. Sometimes when they'd practice, the temperature would be in the fifties.

Fine with Alex.

It was just cool enough to offer some relief when they worked up a sweat during practice. Way different than having to sit in the stands at Heinz Field mid-December in freezing temperatures. Before those frigid days arrived, she'd take advantage of the cool air, the changing leaves, and not having to bundle up in winter gear.

The Owls had a bye week before their game against the Carrolton Saints. But the Steelers were playing at home that weekend against the Packers. That meant seeing Aaron Rodgers in person. The Packers didn't come to Pittsburgh every year the way Lamar Jackson and the Ravens did. So this was like a bonus for Alex, getting to see her two favorite quarterbacks in the same season.

The Packers didn't beat the Steelers this time. But Aaron Rodgers still put on a show in the last minute of the game. Trailing 42–37, he refused to give up until the Steelers recovered an onside kick after Rodgers's last touchdown pass.

The thing Alex loved most about watching the Packers was the way Rodgers's receivers reacted when he had to make a break from the pocket and run for it.

"It's like they all know where to be once he's scrambling around," Alex said to her dad as they headed into the parking lot after the game.

"Every action in football produces a reaction," he replied.

"But that's when it's fun," she said. "When you have to make things up as you go."

"By the way," he said, "what their receivers do? That's what Gabe does when you're in trouble. It's why you two make a great combination."

"On the field," she said.

"You haven't been talking much about him," Jack Carlisle observed. Alex knew her dad would never pry into her personal life, and she could tell he was trying to be respectful of her privacy.

"Nothing much to talk about."

"Maybe you need to talk about it with him."

Alex scoffed. "Believe me, I've tried."

"Lately?"

"No," she said. "But it wouldn't make any difference if I did."

"Maybe it's like when you scramble," her dad said, grinning. "He's just waiting for you to make the first move so he can make one of his own."

They were almost to their car by then.

"What if I do and it doesn't work?" Alex said.

"You won't know until you try."

The next day at school, it was Gabe who made the first move.

Just not in a way that Alex would ever have expected.

Especially not from him.

Sophie had a loose filling, and her mom was taking her to the dentist during lunch. Jabril was in the library, getting some extra studying in before his English test next period. So Alex sat alone. There was a time when that would have made her feel embarrassed or self-conscious or just plain weird. It didn't now. If she'd learned anything from being on the football team, it was that being alone this way, even in a cafeteria full of her classmates, was far from the worst thing in the world.

She just wished she'd brought a book to read.

She was about halfway through her mac and cheese when Lindsey Stiles, Annie Burgess, Mallory Bidwill, and three other girls on the soccer team walked up to her table. *Safety in numbers*, Alex thought.

"Eating with all your friends?" Lindsey said.

Annie, Alex noticed, didn't laugh. But Mallory reacted as if that were the funniest thing anybody had ever said at Orville Middle School.

"Good one, Lindsey," Alex said. "Original. Didn't see that one coming."

There was nowhere for her to go. She wasn't about to give Lindsey Stiles the satisfaction of getting up and walking away. Alex knew it would look as if Lindsey had the upper hand. Like what she said had an effect on Alex. Which it didn't.

Not anymore.

"Sorry," Lindsey said. "You actually *do* have one friend. Where is that loser Sophie?"

Lindsey was always loud, even when she wasn't trying to be. She just had one of those annoying voices that carried from a distance. Alex thought if she weren't so obnoxious, Lindsey would have made a good cheerleader. But one thing never changed with her: when she was talking—and she talked a lot—it sounded to Alex like a fingernail scraping across a blackboard.

Everyone in the cafeteria was watching now.

It had become a show, some free entertainment.

"Here's a heads-up, Linds," Alex said. "The loser isn't Sophie."

"What's that supposed to mean?"

"You'll figure it out," Alex said.

She saw Lindsey's face redden slightly.

"At least I have friends," Lindsey said, arms crossed. "Plural."

"Sure," Alex said. "Keep telling yourself that."

Lindsey bristled. Clearly Alex had struck a nerve. She figured that would be the end of the conversation, but apparently Lindsey had more to say.

"Come *on*, Alex," Lindsey coaxed. "You're the least popular girl in our grade right now. You know who wanted you to go out for the boys' football team? *You* and nobody else."

Alex was preparing a retort when she heard a voice from behind her.

"I did, actually."

She didn't have to turn around to know who the voice belonged to. Even if she hadn't heard it too much lately.

Gabe.

"I'm not talking to you," Lindsey said, scowling at him.

"But it sounded like you were talking on my behalf," Gabe said. "Which you don't get to do."

Lindsey hadn't moved. But her posture seemed to weaken, as if she were figuratively taking a step back.

"This is between Alex and me," she said.

"Well, you and practically half the soccer team," Gabe said, gesturing to the five girls behind her.

If there were kids in the cafeteria who hadn't been watching before, they were now. Though they had to listen extra closely to hear Gabe, who spoke as quietly as he always did.

Alex looked back at Lindsey. It seemed the tables had turned. Now Lindsey was on the defensive. Trying to save face. Alex didn't follow Lindsey Stiles on Instagram. She'd stopped following everybody except Sophie, pretty much. But Lindsey fancied herself the Instagram queen of Orville Middle. Sophie once remarked that Lindsey thought posting what she'd eaten for breakfast that day was fascinating to the rest of the world.

Surely, Alex thought, Lindsey didn't think what was happening now was Insta-worthy. Nevertheless, the entire lunchroom was paying attention.

She wasn't giving up without a fight, though.

"Let me get this straight," Lindsey said. "You're saying you *do* want Alex on the team? Because that's not what my cousin says."

Alex's dad had always taught her that character was something you showed even when nobody was around to see it. But Gabe Hildreth was about to show his now, with most of the school watching.

"He's right," Gabe said. "I didn't at first."

Alex waited.

"But I do now," he said, without a hint of hesitation. "Big-time."

Lindsey opened her mouth. Then closed it. She turned to her teammates, rolling her eyes. "This is boring," she said. "Let's get out of here."

The other girls followed her lead, but Annie slowed, glancing back at Alex until they locked eyes.

Something passed between them, but Alex couldn't pin down exactly what. Then Annie turned and rejoined the group.

Alex watched them go, a mix of pride and relief settling in.

Though, just when she thought the curtain had fallen on their little show, Lindsey was back for an encore.

She turned before she got to the door, raising her voice, although it truly wasn't necessary. "What's it like needing a boy to fight your battles?"

Alex laughed. "Lindsey," she said. "You wouldn't recognize true friendship if it bicycle-kicked you in the face."

Lindsey had no comeback for that. She huffed and led the other girls out of the cafeteria.

As she did, Gabe sat down across from Alex.

And it was as though nothing had ever changed between them.

31

Sophie and Alex didn't have enough time between classes for Alex to give the play-by-play of what had happened at lunch. And when the bell rang at three o'clock, Sophie had to go straight to cheerleading practice. Alex did the same for football. Coach Mencken had moved up the start time of their practice.

So there was no real dish until they were on the phone after dinner.

"You want to hear more about how I rendered Lindsey utterly speechless?" Alex said.

"I already heard about that, *loser*," Sophie said, calling out the word Lindsey used to describe her earlier. Not that Sophie cared a lick what Lindsey thought. "I want to know what happened between you and Gabe."

"I told you already," Alex said. "We talked."

"I *know* you talked," Sophie said. "I want details. Leave nothing out. I've got all night."

"This has to stay between us," Alex said, "even though Gabe didn't strictly forbid me from telling anybody."

"My lips are sealed," Sophie said.

"Your lips are never sealed!"

"You know they are on the big stuff," Sophie said. "So what did he say?"

"He apologized," Alex said.

"He did?" Sophie said. "Wow. Consider *me* speechless."

"I know, right?" Alex said. "He told me he was sorry he hadn't been the kind of friend I deserved."

Alex filled her in on more of the details.

"I think that's probably the most Gabe's spoken all year," Sophie said.

"Or possibly ever," Alex said.

"Maybe he's been saving up for the right moment," said Sophie. "Lindsey must have been stunned."

"Honestly, no one was more stunned than I was."

"Tell me more," Sophie said.

Alex said she told Gabe he didn't need to apologize, but he insisted. He told her about all the heat he'd been taking from Jeff and Lewis and the other guys who lined up with them—though he knew that was no excuse. It was all the same stuff, he said, that Lindsey had been spreading: it wasn't about the team; it was about Alex Carlisle, the girl wonder. The guys were constantly in Gabe's ear, practically forcing him to choose sides. Saying he was either with them or against them.

"Every time Gabe would try to vouch for me, they'd tease him."

"About what?" Sophie said.

"They'd say, 'What is she, your *girlfriend*?'"

"Typical," Sophie said, disgusted. "They make it sound worse than having their bikes stolen."

"Before we left the cafeteria, I told Gabe if the whole school wasn't talking about us before, they would be now."

"What did he say?"

"He said he didn't care," Alex said. "That he never should have cared what other people were thinking or saying, and the rest of the way, he just wants us to play football. He wants us to be the best team we can be. And that only an idiot couldn't see that our best chance at that is with me at quarterback."

"Then what happened when you guys got to practice?" Sophie said.

"We just practiced, like always. The only difference was that Gabe and I stopped trying to avoid each other. We didn't go out of our way to act all chummy. But I think we're cool now."

"What about Jeff?"

"Same old," Alex said. "Every time I catch him looking at me, it's like he's trying to glare me back onto the soccer team."

"He needs to get a life," Sophie said.

"All bark and no bite," Alex agreed.

There was a pause.

"So you forgave Gabe, basically," Sophie said.

"I told you," Alex said. "There was nothing for me to forgive. It's not like he stole my bike."

Sophie giggled. Then in an overly dramatic tone, she said, "What is he . . . your *boyfriend*?"

They both had a good laugh.

THE GAME AGAINST THE CARROLTON SAINTS TOOK PLACE ON THE field at their district high school. It was the first time all season that the Owls would play on turf instead of real grass.

Alex, Gabe, and Jabril were warming up together again. A team within a team.

During stretches, Alex asked them if playing on turf made them feel faster. She'd never played on turf. Not even for soccer.

Jabril smiled. His smile always seemed to be a little bigger on game days.

"The only way I could be faster on a football field," he said, "is if I were riding a motorcycle."

Gabe looked at Alex.

"Faster maybe," he said, "but not more modest."

What happened next was that they fell behind fast. By two touchdowns.

The Saints were good. Really good. Not to mention their guys were some of the biggest Alex had seen all season. They didn't just look as if they belonged on a high school field. They looked ready to play in a high school *game*.

Their quarterback, Andrew Kinsler, was no exception. He also played linebacker but was a much better runner than he was a passer. That much was clear after the first quarter. His arm wasn't as strong as he was, but he was accurate enough with his short passes. He threw one for the Saints' first touchdown, after they'd recovered a fumble due to a botched handoff between Jeff and Tariq. He ran for their second touchdown after Jeff threw an interception deep into the Saints' territory, and they went on a long drive that took them all the way down the field.

Before the second quarter started, Coach told Alex he was putting her in.

"We're in the same kind of ditch as we were for the Cardinals game," Coach said.

"But this time we've got more time to get out of it," Alex said.

"Let's get right after it and see what we can do," Coach said.

The first-down play he wanted was a pass to Gabe on the outside. Then a pitch to Tariq. Then another pass to Gabe on a slant.

She completed her first pass to Gabe, and Tariq gained eight yards on the sweep. First down. Next, she threw low to Gabe, and he went into his slide at just the right moment to make the catch. Another first down. They were moving the chains, moving the ball.

Jake brought in the next play, a deep ball to Gabe down the middle. But Alex never had the chance, or the time, to get the ball to him. Her blockers picked up every one of the guys blitzing her, except one: Andrew Kinsler.

He came from her blind side and just leveled Alex. She was proud that after a hit like that she was able to hold on to the ball. When she looked up, Andrew was standing over her. Not saying anything. Not taunting her. Just looking down.

Then he stuck out a hand, as if to help her up. But just as Alex reached up to take it, he pulled his hand away and sauntered off.

"Go home and put on a dress," he said.

Alex rolled back onto the ground . . .

And began laughing uncontrollably.

That stopped Andrew Kinsler, who turned around and said, "You laughing at me?"

Alex jumped up.

"You know what, dude?" she said. "I guess I am."

"You'll be laughing yourself right off the field when you lose," he said.

"We'll see," was all Alex said.

The ref stepped in then to break up their bickering. Alex thought about telling the ref she wasn't the one who started it. But she was afraid she'd sound dumber than Andrew Kinsler.

Tariq, who'd gotten a quick breather, brought in the next play, a screen pass to him.

"Good," Gabe said.

"Why?" Alex said.

"You'll see."

Alex dropped back, let the rush come to her like you were supposed to on a good screen pass, turned to her left, and threw the ball to Tariq. He was on Gabe's side of the field, which turned Gabe into one of his blockers.

And as Tariq crossed the line of scrimmage, Alex saw why Gabe was eager to run the play. He waited for just the right moment as Andrew Kinsler chased Tariq, then Gabe threw the best block on him any of the Owls had made all season. It was clean, it was legal, Gabe driving his helmet into Andrew's midsection and sending him flying.

By the time Tariq stopped running, he'd gained twenty yards. On the next play, Alex handed the ball to Perry Moses, who ran through a hole in the middle of the line wide enough for a tractor trailer and scored. It was 13–6. Alex threw it to Gabe for the conversion, making it 13–7.

Suddenly things were looking up.

On their way off the field, Alex said to Gabe, "Got a good feeling about this one."

Gabe winked. "Look who's cocky," he said, smiling.

"More like confident," said Alex.

On the Saints' next series, it was Jabril who put Andrew on the ground, causing a fumble that Jabril scooped up and ran in for another Owls touchdown. Alex made a great fake to Tariq on the conversion play, hid the ball beautifully on her hip, ran free into the end zone.

It was 14–13, Owls.

They scored two more offensive touchdowns in the second half. By the end of the fourth quarter, it was Jeff Stiles who got to come in as quarterback at the end of a blowout game. The Owls won 27–13.

The Owls gathered up their water bottles and towels and headed toward the locker room.

All but Alex and Jabril.

They sat on the sideline together, while the parents and coaches talked.

"That guy really told you to go home and put on a dress?" he said in disbelief.

"Yeah."

"So dumb."

"I told him."

Jabril smiled and said, "You even got a dress?"

Alex punched him gently in the arm.

"You don't always have to stay behind with me, you know," she said. "I'm sure you'd rather be in the locker room with the guys."

"Well, as team captain," Jabril said, all proud, "I feel it's my responsibility to make sure you're not feeling left out."

Alex's stomach sank. "Oh, um. Yeah, that makes sense, I guess," she said softly.

Jabril burst out laughing. "Oh man, you really believed that, huh?" Now he elbowed her in the side.

"No, I don't know," she said, half smiling now. "But if I were you, I'd want to be in there with everyone else."

"You should know by now that I do what I want," Jabril said, "and what I want is to talk about the game with our star QB."

Alex gave him a doubtful look. "Star QB, huh?"

"You know it," he said. "Plus, I don't wanna hear Jeff whining in there. Dude gives me a headache."

Alex snickered. Then Jabril leaned over and banged helmets with her, just like he did with the boys.

33

IF THEY WON THEIR NEXT TWO GAMES, THEY WERE IN THE championship. Depending on how the other teams did, they might be able to get in by winning just one.

Nobody on the Owls was thinking that way.

Somehow, through the season's ups and downs, they hadn't lost a game since their opener. They might not have come together off the field the way Alex had hoped, but on it, they'd certainly found their groove. She'd come to accept the fact that she was never going to win over all the guys on the team, or even most of them.

But they were winning. And that wouldn't have happened without her. For now, that would have to be enough. A few weeks ago, she didn't think she'd make the team, let alone get to play. Now here she was, leading the Owls in victory after victory. It surprised her probably as much as it had anybody else. Her coach, her teammates, the guys from opposing teams. Maybe even her dad. She knew she could compete with the boys, on a level field, which was all she'd ever wanted.

Now there was proof.

This wasn't just the way she wanted sports to feel. It was how she wanted to feel about herself. She could live with the classmates who didn't like her. She could tolerate the haters if she had to. She'd thought she'd lost Gabe along the way. But she hadn't.

And maybe the best thing that had happened, away from the field at least, was her friendship with Sophie Lyons. As much of a cheerleader for the Owls as she was for Alex, it was really Sophie who'd become like a sister to her.

She was thinking about all these things in her room a week after the game against Carrolton, the night before their final practice leading up to the Washington Falls game, when the doorbell rang. Alex jumped off her bed before she heard her dad yell up from downstairs that he had it.

She came to the top of the stairs anyway and saw Coach Mencken come through the front door.

He and her dad exchanged a few words while Jack Carlisle led him toward the couch in the living room.

They waved Alex over, and she perched on the edge of the armchair where her dad sat, facing Coach.

"Got something I'd like you both to hear," Coach Mencken finally said.

They all chatted for a few minutes, Coach Mencken telling them that he'd never experienced a football season quite like this. And that a lot of it had to do with his old friend Jack's daughter.

Jack Carlisle smiled and patted Alex's knee with pride.

"Man, there's been a lot going on with this team that has nothing to do with the kids," Coach said.

"How do you mean?" Alex's dad said.

"A lot of the early nonsense about Alex has subsided because we're going good," Coach said. "But you can't believe the noise I'm still getting from the parents."

"Any in particular?" Jack Carlisle said, knowing full well who it had to be.

"Bob Stiles has just been wearing me out," Coach Mencken said. "It's why I had to finally tell him he couldn't be near the field during practice or games."

Now that he mentioned it, Alex realized she hadn't seen Mr. Stiles near the field in a while. It never occurred to her why.

"Bob has pretty much accused me of trying to ruin his son's life," Coach said.

"By making him split time with Alex," her dad said.

"He thinks his boy would be the second coming of Tom Brady if I'd just leave him out there," Ed Mencken said. "Thinks that Alex's presence on the team is what's holding back the boy's development. Top of that, he says the other boys have taken to making fun of Jeff on account of him not being able to beat out a girl."

"What did you say to that?" Alex's dad said.

"I had to tell him that if his son *had* beat out Alex, she wouldn't have gotten the chance to beat *him* out," Coach said.

Alex watched him rub the back of his hand across his forehead. This wasn't the tough-talking, intimidating coach she saw on the field. He didn't sound like a coach at all, just an average guy dealing with his own problems. Like Alex had been dealing with her own.

"Which brings me to why I'm here," he said.

He took a deep breath, let it out.

"I'm thinking about starting you on Saturday against those boys from Washington Falls," he said.

Alex was worried both Coach and her dad might hear her heart beating inside her chest or notice the blood rushing to her cheeks.

"It's not just me trying to do right by you," he said. "I got to do right by everyone on the team. They deserve to have their best chance at winning this thing. And you give us our best chance. Not just when we're coming up from behind."

He nodded at Jack Carlisle and continued. "It's a short season now. And if during these next few games we get behind and don't come back, that would be on me, not doing my job."

He ran a hand through his hair this time.

"I'm not one of those coaches who think winning is the be-all and end-all," he said. "But it's like I tell all our players before every game: the other team is gonna want to win. We're allowed to want to win, too."

Alex knew he was right. Jabril had told her he thought she should be starting, especially since their last two regular season games were against good teams. They were about to come up against some of the strongest teams in the league. It wasn't much of a game plan to fall behind by two losses when they were so close to the championship. They'd been through too much and come too far not to have their best players on the field from the start.

"I didn't want to do anything until I came over and talked to you first," Coach said.

"And we appreciate that, Ed," Jack Carlisle said.

Coach Mencken focused on Alex now.

"So, what do you think?" he said, hands clasped in front of him. He looked at Alex expectantly.

Jack Carlisle peered up at his daughter. The pride in his face made it hard for Alex to say what she was about to say next.

She swallowed, pursed her lips, and looked directly at Coach Mencken.

"Thanks," she said, "but I don't think so."

"You don't think so?" her dad said. "Did we just hear you correctly?"

"Afraid so," Alex said, letting out a breath.

"I don't understand," Coach said, shaking his head. "You *don't* want to start Saturday's game?"

"That's not it," Alex said. "I want to start in the worst way. But I also know it would be the worst thing that could happen to Jeff."

Her dad turned to face her.

"I thought this was what you wanted," he said, his voice soft. "Don't let Jeff Stiles get in the way of achieving your dreams."

Alex stood up and walked to the other side of the coffee table.

"I'm better when I move," she said, looking at her dad. "What's that movie you love where the guy says that?"

"*Butch Cassidy and the Sundance Kid*," he said. "A classic."

She paced back and forth, collecting her thoughts, like buying time on the field after getting forced outside the pocket.

Trying to make the right call.

"I know he's acted like a jerk," she said. "Jeff, I mean. But I'm past all that now."

Her dad huffed. "Wish I was," he said.

"*Dad*," she said. "Let me finish."

"Okay."

"Coach," she said, "you keep talking about how we're going good as a team, that you don't want to mess with success, even if we have to come from behind sometimes."

Alex locked her hands around the back of her neck just to have something to do with them.

"This would crush Jeff," she said. "And make him hate me more than he already does. He'll probably hate me no matter what. But starting is way more important to him than it is to me, and that's a fact."

"Alex," her dad said quietly, "do you think Jeff would ever consider your feelings this way? Or sacrifice what he wanted for you?"

"No," Alex said.

"So why?" Coach said.

"You might not know this, Coach," she said, "but all I've been hearing from everyone at school is that I've tried to make the season all about me."

"All you did is play your best once I gave you the chance," Coach Mencken said. "Nothing wrong with that."

"But whether I liked it or not, it became about me," she said. She let her hands loose now, smiling as she did. "I guess I'm just trying to be the better person. Better than Jeff has been to me."

"And a better teammate," her dad said.

"That's what I've been all along," she said, "even if most of my teammates don't take the time to notice."

She came and sat back down next to her dad, who kissed the top of her head.

Coach said to Alex, "You know that if I start Jeff on Saturday and he's going good, I'm gonna have to leave him out there. You going to be okay with that?"

"I'll have to be," she said. "Even though it might be hard to swallow that we could be doing better if I were playing."

"Gotta say," Coach said, "this was not the way I saw this conversation going."

Alex shrugged. "I'm never a hundred percent sure what to do on or off the field," she said, "but I'm pretty sure this is the right move."

Coach stood up, looked down at Jack Carlisle and said, "In your life would you have ever done anything like this?"

"Heck no," her dad said. "But that's why Alex is going to grow up to be better than I ever was."

When Coach was gone, Jack said to Alex, "You ever going to tell Jeff what you did?"

"Nah," she said. "He wouldn't understand even if I did."

"You're sure this is what you want . . ."

"It's not about me," Alex said. "It's about the team."

BEFORE THE START OF THE GAME AGAINST THE WASHINGTON FALLS Rams, they could all see Coach having what looked to be a fairly heated conversation with Mr. Stiles down near one of the end zones.

Most of the conversation seemed to be coming from Mr. Stiles's direction, as far as Alex could tell.

"What do you think that's all about?" Alex said to Jabril.

"If I had to guess?" Jabril said. "One man down there *is* the coach of the team. The other man *thinks* he's the coach of the team."

Alex and Jeff hardly ever spoke. They didn't speak at practice, they didn't speak at school, and they certainly never spoke during games. They were practically on different teams, the way they interacted. Which is to say, never. It was like they'd never known each other at all.

Which, Alex supposed, they never really had.

Alex hadn't told Gabe or Jabril about Coach's trip to her house. She hadn't told Sophie, either, and she wasn't planning on telling her mom. At least not until after the season was over. Alex was pretty sure her mom wouldn't understand why Alex had turned down the starting job. Liza Borelli believed all women should have the jobs they were qualified to have. Alex agreed, but in this scenario, she felt it wouldn't do her, or the team, any good.

So Alex had one more secret.

One more to add to the growing list.

This secret fell just below the one she held closest to her heart. The one she thought about more than anything else: the desperate need for her mother to see her play.

"These guys are good," Jabril said.

Alex knew he meant the Rams, their opponent in the game about to begin at Washington Falls Junior High. Washington Falls was a big town. Jabril knew a lot about their league and said the field at the junior high was almost as good as the one at the high school.

"You always think whoever we play is going to be as good as the Patriots," Alex said to him, knowing Jabril was prone to exaggerating.

"I like to follow the other teams on social," Jabril said. "I pretend I'm scouting them on the internet. It's why I know they got a quarterback almost as good as you."

He grinned.

"I mean, he's good for a dude," Jabril said.

His name was Jayden Brokaw. He was left-handed, tall and skinny, and had a good arm and a lot of speed. Jabril told Alex that Jayden was going to need it, because he planned to be chasing him all over Washington Falls.

But that didn't turn out to be the story of the first quarter. The story of the first quarter was that Jeff Stiles was finally playing like a starting quarterback. Better than he'd played in any game thus far. He was completing short passes to Gabe and Lewis, Jake and Tariq. On one option play, he kept the ball and ripped off his longest gain of the season. The Owls ended up going seventy-five yards on the opening drive, finally scoring on a ten-yard run by Tariq. Jeff fumbled Cal's snap on the failed conversion play. But the Owls were ahead, 6–0.

Jeff clearly thought this was the way things should have been all along. He came off the field high-fiving everybody in sight as if the Owls had just won the championship. When he got to the sideline, he bent down to fill up his water bottle at the cooler and glanced sideways at Alex, making sure she saw him. He didn't say anything. He didn't have to. Alex read him loud and clear.

It was a look that said, *I'm the only quarterback of this team.*

Jabril saw him do it and shook his head.

"One drive and Jeff thinks he's turned into Lamar," he said into Alex's ear.

They both watched as Jeff went behind the bench and pointed toward where his dad was sitting in the bleachers on the Orville side of the field.

Mr. Stiles stood up and yelled at Jeff, "Hope your coach was watching!"

If Coach Mencken heard, he didn't let on.

"That family has one volume," Jabril said.

"Yeah," Alex said, "loud."

Jayden came right back. Now that the game was underway, Alex saw a much stronger arm than the one she'd seen when he was warming up. On third-and-ten from midfield, he threw a deep ball down the left sideline. His fastest wide receiver had a couple of steps on Bryan. It was all he needed. Jayden dropped the ball in like a pro. Score was 6–6. Then Jayden made a great fake to his running back on the conversion play, kept the ball himself, and it was 7–6.

To Alex's surprise, though, and maybe his own, Jeff Stiles responded. And brought the Owls right back.

"This is one of those body-snatcher deals," Jabril said. "'Cause this is *not* the Jeff Stiles we've been seeing all season."

"He must have had games like this last year," Alex said.

"Yeah," Jabril said. *"Last year."*

"Well, looks like last year just turned into this year," Alex said.

"If it did, it might keep you off the field," Jabril said.

Alex knew what he was getting at. Same thing Coach had said back at her house. If Jeff was going good, he'd have no choice but to keep him in the game.

"You know what I always say," she said.

"Long way to go," Jabril answered.

The Owls scored again to make it 12–7, then missed the conversion. But Jayden was still on fire. He scrambled out of the pocket on the Rams' next series, somehow managing to fake out even Jabril, and ran sixty yards for a score. After he completed a pass to his tight end in the corner of the end zone, it was 14–12, Rams. It stayed that way until halftime.

The Owls had been driving right before the half, but Jeff didn't protect the ball well enough when he was under blitz pressure, got stripped, and the Rams recovered.

Alex honestly wasn't sure what Coach would do at halftime,

whether he'd leave Jeff in at quarterback or not. But he ended the mystery pretty quickly.

"He's played well enough to keep playing," Coach said to Alex.

They both knew he was talking about Jeff.

"Totally get it," she said.

"I want to get you in there," he said, almost apologetic.

"I'm not worried about it," she said to him, just because she couldn't think of anything better in the moment.

You knew this might happen, she told herself as she walked down the sideline to stand next to Gabe. Cal was just about to kick off to the Rams.

"What did he say?" Gabe said.

"He's going to hang with Jeff for now," she said.

Gabe nodded. "Makes sense," he said. "Haven't seen Jeff play this well in a minute."

"If it's good for the team, it's good for me," Alex said. She figured stating it out loud would help ease the disappointment of not getting to play. She wasn't regretting her decision. It was self-less, and she did it for the benefit of the team, not the individual. But deep inside, a part of her was angry for not jumping on the chance when she had it.

"Because you're more of a team player than Jeff will ever be," Gabe said.

Two things happened near the end of the third quarter. Both were bad for the Owls. The first was that Gabe rolled his right ankle trying to make a cut in the open field after completing a really good leaping catch over the middle. When he got to the sideline, Cal's dad checked him out and said the injury wasn't serious, assuring him that icing it would have him feeling good as new by tomorrow. But when there's still more game to play, that's the last thing a player wants to hear.

"How about I start icing now and see how I feel toward the end of the game?" Gabe said.

"You can start icing now," Dr. Calabrese said. "But you're still watching the rest of this game from the bench."

Then, just two plays later, Lewis Healey landed hard on his left wrist trying to make a diving catch on third down, going for a ball he had no realistic chance to catch. He ran off the field, cradling his left wrist in his right hand. Dr. Calabrese was having a busy afternoon.

He declared Lewis done for the day.

Just like that, the Owls were down their two best receivers. The punting team took the field, and the offense came off. Alex was trying to think along with Coach. They had a few other guys who had practiced at wide receiver. Tyler Sullivan, for instance, because of his speed. And Alex knew Jabril could take his spot as slot receiver, no problem. He could run *and* catch. She had no doubt that he could also be a star receiver.

The problem, she knew, would be Jeff. He was only comfortable throwing to two guys: Gabe and Lewis. Now both of them were on the bench with the fourth quarter starting.

Gabe got up off the bench, took Alex by the arm, and limped his way over to where Coach was standing.

"Coach," he said. "You should put Alex in."

He said it only loud enough for the three of them to hear.

"I know we're not moving the ball right now," Coach Mencken said. "But Jeff hasn't done anything that would warrant me taking him out of the game."

Gabe said, "I meant put Alex in at *my* position."

Before Coach could say anything, Gabe continued, words pouring out as fast as he could run.

"Trust me on this, Coach," Gabe said. "She knows where everybody is supposed to be on every play we run. And we've played enough games of catch for me to know she can do that, too. Catch, I mean."

Coach beamed, and Alex could tell he believed Gabe. Despite everything that had happened to the Owls in the past few minutes, he seemed to have newfound hope.

Looking to Alex, he said, "Did Coach Hildreth run this by you?"

"I'm hearing it for the first time," she said, "same as you, Coach."

"You willing to give it a try?" Coach said.

"I'm willing to do just about anything to get on that field," she said.

Coach shrugged. "We've got nothing to lose."

Alex shoved her helmet on. "Well, we could lose the game, but I'm going to do everything possible to make sure that doesn't happen," she told him.

Coach waved Jeff Stiles over and told him the plan for when they got the ball back.

"No way," Jeff said.

A beauty to the end, Alex thought.

"What did you say to me?" Coach said.

"I said no way," Jeff said. Alex didn't know where he found the nerve. "This is the biggest game of the year so far. And she hasn't played a single down all year at wide receiver."

Coach put a hand on Jeff's shoulder.

"Couple of things, son," he said. "One is that Alex hadn't played a down at any position before this season. Two: I wasn't asking for your opinion. And if you've got a problem with *my* opinion, I have another quarterback here ready to go in."

That shut him up. Which was hard to do with Jeff Stiles.

"So, are we on the same page *now*?" Coach said.

"Yes, sir," Jeff muttered.

"Thought so," Coach said.

Coach put Jabril in at Lewis's spot. Alex would take Gabe's. But the first time the Owls had the ball, Jeff missed them both badly with pass attempts, even though they were wide open. His second pass was to Jabril, but it came up short.

Over on the sideline, Jeff said to Jabril, "You made your cut too late."

Jabril had turned to get his water bottle off the bench but stopped in his tracks and came back to where Jeff was standing.

"No," he said.

"No what?" said Jeff.

"No, I didn't make my cut too late," Jabril said. "No, you're *not* going to blame me, like I didn't do my job when the truth is you didn't do yours. That cover everything?"

Suddenly Jeff knew what it was like to be the other team's quarterback when Jabril Wise came after you.

"Whatever," he grumbled.

Jabril took a quick drink and then went right back out after a Rams time-out to be with the defense. And the Owls' defense was stellar again. They did what they'd been doing since the Rams took the lead, and held them again.

But it was clear when the Owls had the ball back that Jeff Stiles was no longer up to the circumstances of the occasion, as Alex's dad liked to put it. That was putting it mildly.

Basically, he was choking out there. He threw two more wild incompletions on the next series, one of them so far over Jabril's head that it was nearly intercepted by a safety ten yards behind him.

It was still 14–12, Rams.

But Jabril and the guys on defense held them again.

Two minutes left now.

Still down two.

Coach came over to Alex after Tariq had made a nice return on the Rams' punt, all the way to their forty-eight-yard line.

"I gotta take Jeff out and put you in at QB," Coach said. "I owe it to the rest of the kids."

"Coach," Alex said, "I think I might have a better idea."

36

"KIND OF LIKE IT," HE SAID ONCE SHE'D EXPLAINED.

Then he shook his head, mouth curling up at the sides into a tight grin. "I didn't originally want a girl on my team," he said. "Now I'm letting her act as my offensive coordinator."

"This can work," Alex said.

"You know what else I like?" he said. "You acting like a quarterback even when you're not on the field."

"I'm just acting like an Orville Owl," Alex said to him.

The offense went back on the field. Coach filled Jeff in on the play he wanted him to run on first down.

It wasn't the one Alex had called on the sideline. Not yet.

Fortunately, the first play was a handoff. Jeff didn't have to throw, just put the ball into Tariq's hands. He could at least manage that. But Tariq nearly got tackled in the backfield and was lucky to fight his way to a two-yard gain. They had one time-out left. Coach didn't elect to use it yet. Alex looked down at the clock behind the end zone.

Minute and thirty seconds left now.

Coach gave Jeff one last chance to complete a pass on second down, this time to Alex. But he airmailed another one out of bounds.

Alex looked over at Coach as she jogged back to the

huddle, the clock stopped on the incompletion. He nodded. She nodded.

Now or never.

Alex told Jeff the play.

"Coach thinks this is how we're going to win the game?" Jeff said to Alex.

She didn't tell him it was her idea.

"Just run it," she said. "And Jabril and I will take care of the rest."

"Yeah, man," Jabril said.

Jeff scoffed. "This will never work."

"Attitude," Alex said.

"You don't get to tell me about attitude," Jeff said.

"Dude," Jabril said, "let go of the act already."

There was no time to continue arguing. They had a game to win.

Alex split out to the left, and Jabril went right. Jeff took the snap in the shotgun, turned, and pitched the ball behind him to Jabril, who'd come flying from Jeff's right. Alex waited a beat before taking off behind Jabril, receiving another pitch from *him*.

What Alex's dad liked to call the old double reverse.

It looked like Alex was going to turn the corner and run for the right sideline. It's what was usually done on a double reverse. But it wasn't a run play.

It was now a pass play.

Jabril hadn't even broken stride after tossing the ball to Alex. He was still charging up the left sideline.

Wide open.

The fastest kid on their team was finally getting the opportunity to show off his speed on offense. Showing off his jets, as he liked to say.

There wasn't a defender within fifteen yards of Jabril when Alex pulled up and let the ball go. She knew it was a sweet throw as soon as the ball left her hand. Maybe the sweetest since she'd won Simba at the fair. The only thing that could possibly have gone wrong was Jabril dropping the ball.

He didn't.

He gathered the ball in with both hands and cruised the last twenty yards into the end zone. It was 18–14, Owls. Tariq ran right behind Cal for the conversion. 19–14, Owls.

That would be the final score.

They were one win away from the championship game. Once again, it didn't matter who had started the game for the Orville Owls.

Just who had finished it.

In style.

37

Before Alex knew it, the Friday before the championship game had arrived.

The Owls had beaten the Lenox Jaguars the previous Saturday with hardly any drama or sweat. The Lenox game turned out like many others the Owls had played down the stretch: Jeff struggling early, Alex coming in for him at the start of the second quarter. Then the next four times the Owls had possession, they scored every time.

By the middle of the fourth quarter, they were winning, 26–6. It was here that Coach put Jeff back on the field and let him finish off a blowout game, the way Alex used to.

Orville Middle had scheduled a pep rally during last period on Friday in the gym. Both the football team and the girls' soccer team had championship games the following day. Alex's new team and her old one had made it through the regular season with just one loss each. It made her wonder how things would have played out if she'd stayed with soccer. Would the soccer team have been better and gone undefeated? There was simply no way of knowing. And that was precisely what made sports so exciting for Alex. You could never guess the outcome.

"If the favorites always won and the underdogs always lost, why even suit up?" her dad would say.

But now that she had played almost an entire season, there was something she believed in her heart to be unquestionably true.

Her new team wouldn't have a game tomorrow without her.

She wouldn't dare say that out loud to anyone, for fear of sounding conceited.

But inside, she delighted at the thought.

On the bus ride to school, she told Sophie she'd never been to a pep rally before and wasn't sure what to expect.

"Well," Sophie said, "the stars will be the cheerleaders, of course."

"Of course," Alex said.

"We'll do some of our totally awesome cheers," Sophie said. "Then the principal will say a few words."

"A *few*?" Alex said. They both knew Principal Ross was notorious for droning on way longer than necessary.

"Fingers crossed," Sophie said. "Then both coaches will speak and call out some of their star players and talk about how they helped the team make it this far. Jabril will get to say something, as captain of your team. And Annie will do the same for the soccer team."

"Bet Jabril's excited about that," Alex said.

"More like thrilled," Sophie said.

"Finally," she continued, "the cheerleaders will come out one last time and get everybody so fired up that both teams will go out tomorrow and win championships."

"Piece of cake," Alex said.

"Cake is probably the one thing that could make this pep rally any better," Sophie said. "It's gonna be awesome!"

Alex could see how pumped Sophie was to get the rally started. Her enthusiasm was contagious. Alex could feel herself getting psyched for the game tomorrow just by being in Sophie's presence.

Later that day, once all the seventh graders had filed into the gym, Sophie and the cheerleaders assembled at the center of the floor and started up with a few simple chants. Alex felt the school spirit in the gym along with everybody else—it was impossible not to. Everyone was wearing school colors and shaking blue-and-white poms.

The girls on the soccer team hadn't changed their attitude toward Alex, even though they'd made it to the championship without her. Things were pretty much the same, especially at lunch. Alex sat with Sophie, Gabe, or Jabril on most days. Sometimes she sat alone.

Maybe it was wishful thinking, but she told herself that things would improve once both seasons were over.

But what if things didn't change?

Her mom often explained to her that when you made choices, you had to live with them.

Liza Borelli had made significant life choices. She never defended them but always recognized that there were pros and cons to each one.

Alex was thinking about her mom now, as Sophie and the cheerleaders ran enthusiastically off the gym floor and sat cross-legged in a row along the baseline. She couldn't lie to herself and say she was happy with the choice her mom made to leave her and her dad behind. But she was forced to accept that choice regardless. Thinking now about what she'd been through this season—was *still* going through—made her at least acknowledge her mom's perspective in a new way.

Still, their relationship was less than ideal. She wished her mom had been around to see Alex chase her own dream. But she wasn't. That was part of the choice she'd made, too. Alex had to respect it.

She just wished the girls she'd once played soccer with had respected hers.

Principal Ross stepped to the microphone now, asking everybody to give the cheerleaders one more round of applause and reminding them that the squad was on their way to the state championships for cheerleading in a few weeks. Then she launched into a long speech about how sports bring the school together.

Next to Alex, Jabril leaned over and whispered, "Well, maybe not the *whole* school."

"Hush," Alex said.

Then it was Coach Mencken's turn. He talked about how proud he was of his team and the way it came together despite some difficult times early in the season.

Please don't mention me, Alex thought.

Thankfully, he didn't.

Afterward, Alex's old soccer coach, Mrs. Williams, said she was proud of her players and praised them for stepping up to face new challenges this year.

Finally, it was Jabril's turn.

By the way he walked up the center aisle, almost skipping,

Alex knew whatever he said was going to be great. Sitting next to her, he'd been a little jittery, but not from nerves. More from anticipation.

And he didn't disappoint.

He stepped up to the microphone, smiled, paused, then leaned forward and shouted, *"Jabril Wise . . . in . . . the . . . house!"*

Everybody cheered.

Jabril cupped a hand to his ear to encourage them to cheer louder.

The volume in the gym reached new heights.

"Now, I'm not much for talking," Jabril said.

A roll of laughter, then someone in the crowd yelled, "Yes you are!"

Jabril laughed, too.

"But I'm up here on behalf of my teammates," he said, "to say that we've done everything great teams should do. We've overcome stuff." Now he paused, just briefly. "Some more than others. But we didn't let anything stop us. We've come from behind. Players got hurt, they came back. Now we've got one more hill to climb."

His voice grew louder now, clearly relishing the moment and building to a big finish.

"Do you all think we're gonna do it tomorrow?"

"Yes!" the crowd roared.

Jabril cupped a hand to his ear one more time.

"I . . . can't . . . hear . . . you!" he yelled.

The screams echoed through the gym.

He walked off and came back down the center aisle, slapping

kids five all the way to his seat. When he sat back down, he said to Alex, "Was I good?"

"Eh," she said with a quick shrug, "I've seen better."

"Over the top, huh?" he said.

She grinned. "Over-the-top *awesome*."

Annie Burgess's turn now.

There was one thing Alex really liked about her former team: they had voted Annie captain and not Lindsey Stiles. No co-captains. Just Annie. Although Alex had heard Lindsey fought tooth and nail for the job. It was a little silly, Alex thought, but Lindsey loved to be in control. After all, she'd managed to get the other girls to join her campaign against Alex. Acting like a leader, if for all the wrong reasons. To her credit, she'd gotten Annie to go along with her, even reluctantly. In that way, Annie had been a follower. But it was obvious to her teammates that she was a born leader on the soccer field.

Annie stepped to the microphone now.

"Hi," she said. "I'm Annie Burgess, and if you know me, you know I'm way better at kicking a ball than public speaking. But I just want to take this time to thank my teammates for supporting me this season and to thank all of you for the way you've supported us. I hope we don't let you down tomorrow."

There was a nice round of applause. Nothing like the response for Jabril. Then again, it was hard for anyone to measure up to Jabril.

But Annie wasn't through.

"I'd like to say one more thing before the cheerleaders come back up," she said once the applause died down. "It doesn't just have to do with soccer."

Annie stood close enough to the microphone that everyone could hear her inhale deeply. Alex waited with the rest of the crowd, unsure of what was coming next.

"Principal Ross said that sports can bring us together," Annie said. "And they can. They just haven't at our school this fall."

She took another breath.

"But there's someone in this gym who used to be my teammate, and she did something great on her new team," Annie said. "Our team should have been behind her. Everybody should have been behind her. I wasn't, and that's on me."

The gym had gotten very quiet.

"You know who should be up here today getting cheered?" she said. "Alex Carlisle."

Another breath for Annie.

Alex held hers.

"Alex did something incredible. She was good enough to play quarterback on the football team, and she did exactly that. But too many of us turned our backs on her." Annie gestured to the crowd.

"There's not a person in this gym who hasn't been told they can achieve anything if they work hard enough. Well, Alex worked her butt off and showed us all what grit and perseverance can do. And I think that's pretty cool."

Alex glanced down her row and saw Gabe's jaw drop. Her own wasn't too far behind.

Then Annie looked over toward Alex and said, "I can't speak for everyone. But from me to you, Alex, I'm sorry."

Alex nodded her head at Annie to acknowledge the apology,

hoping Annie wouldn't ask her to come up. For someone who hated being the center of attention, that would be more than Alex could endure.

What Annie Burgess did instead was start to clap. Jabril and Gabe were the first to join, and slowly, some of the other kids did the same. Alex ducked her head. It would be super embarrassing if only a handful of kids applauded her in a gym full of hundreds. But soon, the sound began to amplify until it overwhelmed the room. There were probably a few stragglers, but that hardly mattered to Alex.

So many of them had gone along with the crowd early in the school year. Now they did it a different way. A better one. Jabril threw an arm around Alex and gave her shoulder a squeeze.

"Shoulda been like this from the start," he said.

38

THE PALMER LIONS HAD LOST TO ONLY ONE TEAM: THE OWLS. So even though both teams were tied with one loss, that head-to-head win was the reason the championship game would be played at Orville Middle. The Owls had earned the home field advantage.

But when Alex, Gabe, and Jabril checked the Lions' record, the scores showed that they had rolled over most of their opponents the way the Owls had rolled over them.

"They're going to want payback," Alex had said to Gabe and Jabril on Friday night.

"Doesn't scare me," Jabril said.

"Explain, Wise Man," Gabe said.

"First of all, it's the championship game, so nobody needs extra motivation," Jabril said. "And second? They can want payback all they want, but they remember the beating we already gave them, same as we do."

The kickoff was scheduled for eleven o'clock the next morning. Alex woke up at seven without having to set her alarm. Her dad had left her jersey folded on the seat of her chair and her gear on the desk. Jack Carlisle liked to be organized. Lying in bed, Alex looked at the helmet she'd left sitting on Simba's head and remembered back to the day she and her dad had picked it out at Dick's Sporting Goods.

When her dad poked his head in to see if she was up, he nodded at Simba and said, "Helmet looks much better on you."

"You know what, Dad?" she said. "It fit great in the store. But it suits me better now."

Then she said, "Tell the truth. Did you really think I could do it?"

He leaned against the wall, just inside her bedroom door. "I thought you could be a player," he said. "I just didn't know you'd turn into this kind of player so quickly." Then he paused and said, "What about you?"

"It's weird," she said. "Once I suited up that first day of tryouts, I felt like I belonged. Even if I was the only one who did. Then I had to prove it when I got on the field."

"Which you did."

"Yeah," she said. "I guess I did."

"My girl," he said. "When do you want to head over to the field?"

"Now?" she said.

They both laughed. There had been other big games in Alex's life. She'd played championship games in soccer and softball. They'd just never felt quite like this, with so much at stake.

"You know how proud I am of you, right?" he said.

"Like I know my passwords," she said.

They got to the field at ten. Jabril and Gabe beat her there, so Alex joined their warm-up. Jabril and Gabe jogged out for passes, and Gabe threw a few to Alex, too. All of them were trying to play it cool, as if this were just another game.

Knowing it wasn't even close.

Jabril pointed to the other end of the field, where some of the Lions were beginning to arrive.

"Look," he said, "your friends are here."

Leading the way were No. 14 and No. 58. Alex knew their names now. The quarterback was Sam Pickett. The linebacker was Kenny Vila.

"They're going down," Gabe said.

"We just need to be one point higher on the scoreboard when the game's over," said Alex.

"Gotta start with us," Jabril said. "The Three Musketeers."

They formed a small huddle before joining the rest of their teammates for stretching. Jabril put out his hand in the middle. Gabe placed his on top, and Alex placed hers on top of Gabe's.

"Let's finish what we started," Jabril said.

Right before the kickoff, Coach gave his shortest pregame talk of the season, which meant it only lasted seconds. Alex thought it was his best.

"Took us a while to be the team I wanted us to be," Coach Mencken said. "But now we are. So go be that team today."

Problem was, the last game of the Owls' season started out like their first.

They quickly found out why Sam Pickett and the Lions *had* rolled through the rest of their season after their horrible loss to the Owls. Sam came out mixing passes with runs. His blockers managed to neutralize Jabril on the Lions' first drive, going right down the field and making it look way too easy. It took four minutes in game time. The Owls were able to block the extra point, but when the drive was over, the Lions were ahead, 6–0.

The Owls came back. At this point in the season, they knew they could get back up after getting knocked down. They got back up, mostly running the ball on their own first drive. Jeff attempted only one pass. They were finally facing fourth-and-goal from the four-yard line when Coach called for an option play, with Jeff and Tariq running to their right, Jeff with the option of keeping the ball or pitching it. Jeff saw an opening and decided to keep it. When he got close to the goal line, he launched himself into the air, ball outstretched in front of him.

Kenny Vila, coming from the left, got to Jeff before he crossed the line. He knocked the ball loose, recovering it himself at the Lions' one-yard line.

It was then that everybody noticed Jeff still hadn't gotten up.

He had landed awkwardly on his throwing shoulder. Coach jogged out onto the field, followed closely by Jeff's dad and Dr. Calabrese. Alex saw Dr. Calabrese check Jeff out right away, gently manipulating the shoulder, asking him to make some simple movements with it. After a few minutes, Jeff sat up, and Coach helped him to his feet. From her position on the sideline, Alex saw Jeff pressing his right arm tightly to his stomach as he came off the field.

"The good news is that I think you only bruised it," Dr. Calabrese said. "The bad news, son, is that you're done for the day."

"But that means done for the season, too!" Jeff yelled.

"I know you want to play," Dr. Calabrese said. "But you'd risk turning a bad bruise into something more serious."

Then Mr. Stiles pulled Dr. Calabrese aside, and they walked behind the Owls' bench. As usual, Mr. Stiles did most of the talking. They could hear his voice projecting, muffling Dr. Calabrese's responses, until they heard Mr. Stiles say, "I'm the dad."

"And I'm the doctor," Cal's dad boomed, and walked away.

Alex walked over to Jeff. "I'm sorry," she said. And she meant it, too. This was no way for anybody's season to end. Even his.

Jeff had his helmet off now. His face was red. So were his eyes. Alex thought he might cry.

"No, you're not," he snapped at her.

Alex turned and walked away, thinking that at least Jeff Stiles had been consistent to the end.

The Owls' defense managed to pin the Lions inside their ten-yard line. The Lions' punt only made it to the thirty. Great field position, which Alex immediately squandered. On second down she rolled to her left. This time it was an option for her to run or throw. She attempted a throw, trying to squeeze in a pass to Gabe, who was covered by Kenny Vila. But Kenny read her perfectly. He stepped in front of Gabe, intercepted the pass, and started running the other way. Alex tried to get in his way, but Kenny stiff-armed her, and she fell to the ground. Then there was nothing but open field in front of him. He wasn't as fast as Jabril, but fast enough. It was 12–0. Jabril at least kept it that way by knocking down Sam Pickett's conversion pass.

They were still down two touchdowns.

The score stayed 12–0 until halftime. Nothing Alex tried on

offense during the rest of the first half had worked. The only small victory was recovering her own fumble on the Owls' last play.

As she walked off the field, head down, she thought to herself: *If I'd played like this at tryouts, I wouldn't have made the team.*

She only lifted her head when she heard her name being called from behind the Owls' bench.

There, standing in front of her, was Dr. Liza Borelli.

Mom.

SHE COULDN'T PROVE IT, BUT ALEX WAS PRETTY SURE SHE'D RUN
faster than Jabril in that instant. Slowing down so she wouldn't
crush her mom on impact, she held out her arms and gave her
mom a hug that could have lasted the rest of the game.

When they pulled back from each other, her mom said,
"Surprise."

She was wearing what appeared to be an ancient Orville High
hoodie and jeans. Her hair was in a low ponytail.

"How . . . ?" Alex said.

Then: "Why didn't you . . . ?"

Her mom grinned.

"I'm a doctor," she said. "Things happen with patients. Plans
change. I didn't want to tell you I might be coming and then have
to disappoint you at the last minute."

Alex had casually mentioned on the phone that she wished
her mom could see her play, knowing it was all but impossible. Realistically, she never expected her mom would come.
Never thought she *could*, with her packed schedule at the
hospital. That was the secret she'd kept to herself all this
time. How much she wanted—*needed*—her mom to see her
on the field in person. Alex could never begin to imagine
her mom getting on a plane and flying all the way across the

country to see her daughter play a game of seventh-grade football.

But she had.

And now here she was.

Watching Alex play—poorly—in the big game.

"I was supposed to be here for the start of the game," her mom said. "Took the red-eye. Then we got delayed for a couple of hours because of fog."

"You're here now," Alex said. "That's all that matters. Other than the fact that I stink."

Alex noticed her dad about five yards behind her mom. Giving them room.

"As you know, I'm no football expert," Alex's mom said, facing Alex and reaching across to plant both hands on her shoulders.

"A well-known fact," Alex said.

"But even I know the game's not over yet."

Alex knew it was time to get back with the team. Before she did, she asked her mom, "Any words of wisdom?"

"Play better?" her mom said.

It was basically the same advice they got from Coach Mencken.

"You're all better than this," he said, standing at the center of the large circle they made around him. "Now you've got half a game instead of a whole one to prove it."

The cheerleaders were finishing up their routine at midfield when Coach turned to Alex.

He reminded her they weren't going to make up twelve points on one play.

"Don't try to be anything other than yourself," he said.

"I have to do better than I did in the first half," said Alex.

"What first half?" Coach said with a wink. "As far as I'm concerned, the game starts right now."

Alex took a quick look over her shoulder, to where her mom sat with her dad in the bleachers. Then she went out to play the second half of the big game.

Before the Lions kicked off, Gabe said to Alex, "I saw your mom."

"I'm still in shock," Alex said.

"Time for you to shock those Lions right out of the lead," Gabe said, and pounded her some fist.

Tyler made a nice return of the kickoff, taking the ball all the way to the fifty-yard line. The offense took it from there, putting the first half behind them and starting fresh. Gabe made the biggest play. Alex had taken a direct snap, stood right up, and thrown the ball across the field to Gabe, who caught it fixed in place. Once the catch was made, *then* he made his move, putting such a good fake on Kenny Vila that Kenny ended up on the ground. Gabe finally ran twenty yards all the way to the Lions' eighteen-yard line.

Two plays later Alex dropped a pass in to Gabe over double coverage, right in front of the goalposts. The Owls were on the board. The conversion play was a quarterback draw. Cal and the guys in the line opened a huge hole for Alex, and she sprinted through it.

Now it was 12–7.

After Alex handed the ball to the ref, Kenny Vila came walking over. He'd missed her on the conversion, same as his teammates.

"Enjoy the last points you guys are going to score all season," he said.

"Wanna bet?" Alex said.

Coach had told her to be herself, after all.

It began to rain a few minutes later. By the end of the third quarter, the score still 12–7, the rain was coming down hard. But the wind was practically nonexistent, so when Alex or Sam Pickett could get a good grip on the ball, they threw it fairly accurately.

The challenge was getting a good grip.

It had become a defensive game by then. Jabril seemed to be everywhere. So did Kenny Vila. The Owls had a terrific long drive at the start of the fourth quarter, but then Lewis dropped a fourth-down pass in the end zone that would have put the Owls in the lead.

So it was still 12–7 when the Owls got the ball back, probably for the last time, on their ten-yard line.

Three minutes left.

"I know it's a challenge throwing," Coach said. "But we're gonna have to throw pretty much every down."

Alex felt herself smiling.

"Grip and rip," she said.

Coach leaned down. Alex could see the water dripping off the brim of his *O* cap.

"If you're the player I believe you are," he said, "you'll be that player now."

Alex ran out onto the field with the offense thinking: *Time to be the player I believe I am.*

• • •

"Ninety yards to go," Alex said when she knelt in the huddle, before she told them the plan to run a screen to Tariq.

"Piece of cake," Gabe said.

"I *know* you're not thinking about cake at a time like this," Alex said.

She laughed to herself, thinking of what Sophie had said the day before at the pep rally.

Perhaps if they won, there'd be cake in her future.

But that wasn't her concern right now. Right now, it was about getting across the field and past the goal line.

Though for just a moment, their banter seemed to lighten the mood in the huddle. Alex remembered she'd read something about Joe Montana joking with his teammates during the Super Bowl when they had over ninety yards to go.

She shook out her hands, trying to dry them as best she could. Then she broke the huddle, and when the ball was hiked, she threw a short pass to Tariq. Gabe threw him a big block on the closest Lions defender, and Tariq ran all the way to the thirty-yard line. Jake had thrown an incredible block of his own on Kenny Vila, but Kenny's spike accidentally came down on Jake's hand, and he had to come out.

To Alex's surprise, Jabril came running out to replace him.

"Coach asked if I wanted to join the fun," Jabril said. "Know what I told him?"

"Heck yeah!" Alex said, slapping him a low five.

The play was a pass to Jabril over the middle. The ball slipped coming off Alex's fingers, and it wobbled through the rain. But it got there nonetheless. Jabril caught it and gained ten yards, flattening one of the Lions' safeties along the way.

The rain was coming down harder than ever. Alex messed up a handoff to Tariq, the first running play Coach had called. The ball fell to the ground but somehow bounced right up into Tariq's hands, and he managed to gain five yards. Sometimes it was better to be lucky than good, Alex's dad liked to say.

The Owls finally found themselves on the Lions' twelve-yard line with one minute left in the championship game.

Coach called their last time-out, and Alex ran over to get the first-down play: a pass to Gabe. But when this ball slipped out of Alex's hands, it sailed long and over Gabe's head.

Alex got forced out of the pocket on the next play, having to scramble. She thought she could get to the sideline but didn't and got tackled from behind. The clock was still running.

Third down.

Alex looked over at Coach. He waved at her, as if to say, *Go for it.*

Meaning that Alex should call the play.

Alex knew which play she wanted to run. In the huddle she quickly told her teammates they were going with the pass-run option. It was the same play she'd royally messed up in the first half, the bad pass that Kenny Vila turned into a touchdown.

"Calling your own number," Gabe said.

"Or yours," Alex said.

"Love it," he said. Then he tapped her helmet with his and said, "Do your job."

"Back at you."

She expected the Lions to come at her with an all-out blitz. It's what she would have called if she were in their position. If the Lions could stop the Owls on this play and the next, they would be the champs. If Alex could get her team into the end zone—where Kenny Vila was so positive they weren't going until next season—then the Owls would be the champs.

The Lions blitzed.

Alex wanted to run to her left, but there was no way to do that now. One of the Lions' safeties had gotten around Jabril's block and was flying at her from that direction.

She reversed her field and ran to the right. As she made her cut, the safety slipped and went down.

But he wasn't the only one chasing her. There were a lot of big guys, all of them turning on their jets now, running through the slop.

Gabe had run his pattern to the left. But when he saw that Alex was in trouble, he cut back across the back line, Kenny Vila on his heels and the other Lions safety in front of him.

Alex ran for the sideline again, almost out of room and out of time, thinking about throwing the ball away if she had to and stopping the clock in the process.

The first time they'd run the play today, she'd tried to force the ball in to Gabe, made a bad throw, and gotten run over by Kenny Vila as the play turned into a total disaster.

She wasn't going to let that happen again.

Wasn't going to make a bad throw, not now.

And she wouldn't throw the ball away, either.

As Gabe cut in front of the goalposts, Alex saw that he was open by a margin. Just enough. A small hole, like the one she'd put the ball through at the fair.

She didn't even try to plant a foot in the mud. Alex threw on the run, with the best grip on the ball she'd had the whole second half, throwing it as hard as she could through the rain. Kenny Vila reached in from behind with his right arm, and the safety was a step late reacting to the ball, reaching in from Gabe's left.

The ball hit Gabe in the stomach. He cradled it with both arms, then sat down in the back of the end zone with the winning touchdown.

It was 13–12, Owls.

The lights on the scoreboard glowed.

Right back to where I started, Alex thought as she ran for Gabe.

Make throw.

Win prize.

40

BEFORE THE OWLS AND THEIR PARENTS LEFT TO GATHER IN THE cafeteria for the trophy ceremony, Kenny Vila sought out Alex to shake her hand.

"You're good," he said.

To say Alex was stunned at this peace offering was an understatement. But she didn't let on. Instead, she stuck out her hand and said, "So are you."

He nodded his head, a way of saying things were cool between them, and walked away to join the rest of his team.

The ceremony was brief. Everybody was eager to get home to shower and dry off from the rain. Coach had brought in the trophy and said he'd be sending it out to get inscribed with the names of every player on the team. It would eventually go in the glass showcase near Principal Ross's office.

Then Coach announced that their official team party would be the following week at Bostwick's.

"I'd usually give out a game ball for such an occasion," he said. "But I'd need three today, for Jabril, Gabe, and Alex."

A big applause followed, with hoots and hollers. Alex swore she heard her mom scream, "Yeah, Alex!" above the clamor.

"Three Musketeers," Gabe whispered.

• • •

Later on, Jack hosted a few players and their parents for a post-game party at their house. Jabril and Gabe came over after they went home to change, but Sophie came straight from the field in her cheerleading uniform, which was only now starting to dry.

"You guys killed it out there," she said.

"Piece of cake," Alex said.

Sophie's eyes went wide. "Oh my god, cake!" she said. "You guys totally earned it."

Of course, because it was Jack Carlisle, it was an ice cream cake. He'd brought it home the night before and kept it in the freezer as a surprise. Alex realized he must have bought it knowing it would either be a celebratory cake or a consolation cake. She was glad it was the former.

Alex's dad brought the cake out now, with three lit candles sticking up out of the center. He set it on the island in the kitchen, and everyone gathered around. Alex sidled up next to him.

"Without embarrassing my daughter . . ." he started.

"Oh boy, here we go," Alex muttered, pinching her dad in the side.

"I played football until football finally told me I wasn't good enough to keep playing," Jack said. "And my whole life I dreamed about making the kind of pass my kid made today to win a title."

Alex looked around the room and thought that being the center of attention—when it was for a good reason—wasn't so bad.

"I couldn't be prouder," he said. Then he pointed out the candles. "The number three is significant tonight. First, because that's my girl's number. The triple threat, Alex Carlisle."

Jabril whooped, and others clapped.

"But also because three key players led the Owls to a championship win tonight. And that's Alex, Jabril, and Gabe."

The room went wild.

Then Sophie's voice called above the rest. "Give me an *O!*"

Everyone chanted back, *"O!"*

"Gimme a *W!*"

"W!"

"Gimme an *L!*"

"L!"

"Gimme an *S!*"

"S!"

"What's that spell?"

"OWLS!"

"Who's number one?"

"OWLS!"

Then Alex, Jabril, and Gabe blew out the candles together.

After the crowd dispersed and most people took seats in the living room, Alex found herself alone in the kitchen with her mom. Liza Borelli could only stay for the night. She had to fly back to California in the morning. It meant all the more to Alex that her mom flew six hours just to stay for less than twenty-four. It was bittersweet, too. They had very little time to spend together.

"I know I missed a lot in your life," Alex's mom said. "But I'm sure glad I didn't miss this."

"Glad you came, Mom," Alex said. They were sitting on stools opposite each other at the counter.

"Was it worth it?" Alex asked. "The choice you made? When you think about all the stuff you did miss out on?"

Her mom sighed and smiled.

"Been waiting your whole life to ask that question, huh?" she said.

"Maybe it took this season for me to ask it."

"I look back now," Liza Borelli said, "and think that maybe there could have been another way, if I had to do it all over again. If I could have worked harder on my marriage and still been able to become a doctor. Have the life I imagined for myself. But I didn't see a way at the time. So I made the choices I did. Gave up a lot. To get a lot." She shrugged. "Maybe a man wouldn't have had to make the same choices. Who knows? What I know is that I'm happy. And a big part of that happiness—probably the biggest part—is that I'm looking at a pretty happy young woman."

She leaned forward on the table and covered one of Alex's hands with her own.

"Was this season worth it for you?" she asked Alex.

Alex took a few seconds to consider, but knew there was really only one answer.

"Heck yeah!" she said.

"My girl."

EPILOGUE

So that's how it all went down.

I left out some stuff, but nothing all that important.

That's how I got to play quarterback. It's how we won the championship and how I won over some people along the way.

Even if I couldn't win over all of them.

They wanted me to make some kind of speech or whatever at the end of the night, but I told them I'd done most of my talking on the field. Then Jabril got up and told everybody that maybe more football players should woman up. My mom gave Jabril a high five for that one.

But I knew it wasn't about that in the end. Just about being good enough to do the job. No matter who, or what, you are.

In the end, I did say one thing. Because Sophie made me, threatening to do some vaults over the coffee table if I didn't. So I stepped into the middle of the living room, where I'd watched all that football with my dad, never believing I'd get to take the field myself.

Until I started dreaming.

"You know what I can't wait for?" I said.

"More cake?" Sophie guessed.

"Next year," I said.

Wait till you hear about that one.

Read all of Mike Lupica's bestselling novels!